He tightened his hold on her hand and slowly pulled until her face was inches from his. "Your heart rate just sped up and your skin is growing warmer at the thought of our lying on the grass and making love."

She tried to keep her breathing steady. "For a businessman you have such an incredible imagination," she finally forced out.

He smiled. "Is it? Think about it, Kelly—the two of us lying down here on incredibly thick grass, my slipping off your clothes, your taking off mine. Our having the chance to discover what we've missed. While moonlight is great for making love, sunlight is much better."

Liquid desire rushed through her veins as she visualized all he was talking about, arousing her until all she could think of was his body merging with hers. "Ben," she managed to say, "I told you before that it's not a good idea. I'm very confused about what's happening between us, and I'm still trying to understand something I've never experienced before."

"When I'm around you I discover it's not easy to go slow," he said, lowering them to the grass. . . .

WHAT ARE *LOVESWEPT* ROMANCES?

They are stories of true romance and touching emotion. We believe those two very important ingredients are constants in our highly sensual and very believable stories in the LOVESWEPT *line. Our goal is to give you, the reader, stories of consistently high quality that may sometimes make you laugh, sometimes make you cry, but are always fresh and creative and contain many delightful surprises within their pages.*

Most romance fans read an enormous number of books. Those they truly love, they keep. Others may be traded with friends and soon forgotten. We hope that each LOVESWEPT *romance will be a treasure—a "keeper." We will always try to publish*

*LOVE STORIES YOU'LL NEVER FORGET
BY AUTHORS YOU'LL ALWAYS REMEMBER*

The Editors

Loveswept 643

SUDDEN IMPULSE

LINDA WISDOM

BANTAM BOOKS
NEW YORK · TORONTO · LONDON · SYDNEY · AUCKLAND

SUDDEN IMPULSE
A Bantam Book / October 1993

*If you would be interested in receiving protective vinyl
covers for your Loveswept books, please write to this
address for information:*

*Loveswept
Bantam Books
P.O. Box 985
Hicksville, NY 11802*

ISBN 0-553-44254-6

Published simultaneously in the United States and Canada

Bantam Books are published by Bantam Books, a division of Bantam
Doubleday Dell Publishing Group, Inc. Its trademark, consisting of the
words "Bantam Books" and the portrayal of a rooster, is Registered
in U.S. Patent and Trademark Office and in other countries.
Marca Registrada. Bantam Books, 1540 Broadway, New York,
New York 10036

PRINTED IN THE UNITED STATES OF AMERICA

OPM   0 9 8 7 6 5 4 3 2 1

ONE

Ben Wyatt was looking for a woman. Not just any woman, but a special one. A woman who had teased his senses even though he'd never met her, never even seen her.

But he could picture her in his mind. Petite, long blonde hair, big blue eyes, and the smile and demeanor of a fairy tale princess. Someone with delicate features, the kind of woman a man cherished and protected from the harsh outside world. She was his quest.

And a grizzled individual known as Cap'n Jack was revealing just where he could find that woman.

"Whaddya want her for?" Cap'n Jack,

who had several days' growth of beard, sun-toughened skin, faded blue eyes, and cotton pants and shirt that had seen better days, surveyed Ben's neatly pressed khaki slacks and dark green polo shirt with a bit of disdain.

"Business." He hid his impatience as the man continued to look at him. It appeared Cap'n Jack wasn't about to reveal anything without a good reason. "My shops sell her hand-painted clothing."

"Oh, yeah, I heard she does real well with those. 'Course, you'd never catch me wearing one of those fancy shirts with flowers and fish painted all over them." The man looked off into the distance. "Did you ask up at the hotel?"

"That was the first place I went to. They told me where she lives and I tried there, but was told by two little boys she wasn't there and was in town."

"You try Lili's? She owns the—"

"Yes, I was told she was probably down here on the dock."

The man smiled. "Could be. I haven't seen her for maybe three days, so it would be about time."

Ben had already decided he wouldn't get

anything more from this old man from the sea. He'd called Kelly Andrews before he'd left Sydney to set up a meeting with her while he was making the rounds of his South Seas clothing boutiques, but she'd merely asked if there were any problems with her merchandise and said that if not, she was sorry but she wouldn't have the time to see him.

But being the stubborn Aussie he was, he wasn't about to be put off like a door-to-door salesman. It had meant a trip to Treasure Cove, a small island that did a more than reasonable business thanks to a luxury resort that catered to wealthy clients who wanted the white sands, the hot Pacific sun, and a great deal of privacy, but he was more than willing to make an extra stop if it achieved his purpose.

"Did you try the Rusty Nail?" Cap'n Jack's words penetrated Ben's thoughts.

"Rusty Nail?"

Cap'n Jack nodded, using his pipe to point the way. "Down there at the end of the dock. You can't miss it. It's Tuesday, so she's probably there doing the books." He nodded as he lifted the pipe to his lips and puffed energetically. "Yep, I bet that's where you'll find her."

"And if not?"

He shrugged. "Can't say. You're an Aussie, ain't ya?"

"Yeah, I am."

"Thought so. The men come out here for the fishing while the wives and girlfriends stay up by the pool or on the beach. Like I said, try the Rusty Nail. Just bet you'll find Kelly there. But let me give you a word of advice, son: Don't put the moves on her. Kelly's frosted the best."

Ben's lips quivered with anticipation. The more he heard about the elusive Kelly Andrews, the more she fascinated him. "Thanks. I'll keep your advice in mind."

"And don't drink the house-brand whiskey," Cap'n Jack called after him. "The stuff'll melt your stomach."

"Damn island's as bad as a small town," Ben murmured, walking in the direction Cap'n Jack had indicated. A row of typical waterfront stores ended with a weathered building and an equally weathered sign hanging outside indicating it was the Rusty Nail, purveyor of spirits and wines.

Once he got inside, he felt as if he'd stepped onto the set of a forties adventure film. The room was predictably smoke-filled, the jukebox—which he swore was an authentic Wurlitzer, complete with bubbling lights—played music from the World War II era, and muted sounds of various conversations were punctuated with spurts of profanity that strained the imagination. All this, along with the exterior dilapidation, added up to a picture of a typical waterfront tavern. Ben wouldn't have been surprised to see Clark Gable or Errol Flynn sitting at one of the tables.

Even the bartender, who was drawing beer, looked as if he belonged in the same film, with his tattoo-covered arms as big as tree trunks, hands the size of hams, and a nose that looked as if it had been broken so many times Ben wondered if the man still had a sense of smell.

Ben stood to one side of the entrance and looked around. He convinced himself he wouldn't find Kelly in these crude surroundings. Not after the mental picture he'd nurtured. But it was worth a try. Now that it was time to meet the real woman, he wanted more than ever to see how close she came to his mental image.

"This ain't the Sheraton, friend," said a burly man as he staggered over to Ben. The man smelled strongly of fish and the yeasty aroma of a few too many beers, and was eyeing Ben with a great deal of suspicion.

Ben figured this was the perfect time to name-drop and see what would happen. "I was told to meet Kelly Andrews here."

The suspicion melted immediately. "She's over in the corner."

Ben turned around. He saw women sitting at three corner tables. None of them looked like the Kelly he'd been visualizing, although one did appear to be someone he wouldn't mind getting to know. "Which one?"

The man frowned at him as if Ben was the one not seeing straight, then cocked his thumb over his shoulder. "The one wearing sort of a brown shirt."

Ben followed the man's gesturing thumb and felt as if a lead weight had been slammed against his stomach. *She* was Kelly Andrews? Although she wasn't petite and blonde, he didn't feel the least bit disappointed. The reality was better than anything his imagination could have conjured up.

She was seated, but he could tell she was fairly tall. The soft cinnamon-colored shirt displayed full breasts and accented lightly tanned skin. Hair the color of honey was piled on top of her head in a loose knot and eyes the same tawny color were watching the goings-on. Right now, those all-seeing eyes were on him. They didn't change expression as he walked toward her.

"Ms. Andrews, I'm Ben Wyatt." He held out his hand.

She didn't move, she didn't smile, and she didn't take his hand. She just continued watching him with those seductive eyes, eyes that were suddenly downright chilling.

"Yes, I heard you've been looking for me, Mr. Wyatt." Her voice was a husky contralto.

"You didn't make it easy."

"Perhaps because I didn't care to be found." She didn't turn away and she didn't offer him a seat. He took one anyway.

"Even when there's business to be discussed?" He noticed that the Sherman tank who was doubling as the bartender was making his way toward them.

He stood behind Ben's chair, then asked, "Want I should get rid of him, Kelly?" in a gravelly voice with an accent straight out of Brooklyn.

The smile she directed at the bartender made Ben think of a tiny kitten toying with a grizzly bear. "No, Del, it's fine. Would you please send over a whiskey for Mr. Wyatt?" she requested.

The man nodded, then waved a meaty finger at Ben. "Nobody hurts Kelly," he warned before lumbering off.

"Quite a protection ring you have here, Ms. Andrews," Ben said lightly. He couldn't keep his gaze from wandering over her face. He was used to women who refused to leave the bedroom, much less the house, without full makeup on, and her touch of dark mascara and deep peach lipstick was a nice change of pace. She was proof a woman didn't need tons of cosmetics to look lovely. "But I guess in a place like this you would have to be careful of being approached."

Kelly merely inclined her head, not saying yes or no. "The Rusty Nail does have a reputation for brawls. The locals like it because they can come in here off their boats and no one looks at them as if they're barbarians. The hotel guests prefer their drinks with little umbrellas and skewers of pineapple sticking out of the glass."

Ben's gaze fell on the record-keeping books laid out in front of her. "I should think your hand-painted clothing would pay you enough that you wouldn't have to worry about a second job."

"I do well," she said cryptically. "This is just another facet of my life." She swept her arm outward.

Now it all fell into place. "The Rusty Nail is yours."

"Lock, stock, and beer barrels." She waited until Del set the squat glass in front of Ben. "Thanks, Del. Mr. Wyatt is a business associate," she explained.

Ben hoped that was meant in a positive way.

Del didn't look convinced. "Right."

Ben lifted the glass and took a cautious sip. Kelly's lips curved. "Since you're with me, Del wouldn't dare serve you the house brand, which is actually a private joke among the locals."

"Just checking."

Now Kelly was able to take a little inventory of her own. Actually, she had started looking Ben over the moment he'd entered the tavern. She'd known his identity from the first. Occasionally, a tourist would stumble in, take one horrified look, and practically run out. Ben hadn't even flinched when Kane, probably smelling of fish as he always did, had

walked up to him. This was a man to be reck-
oned with.

She'd marked men off her list of personal wants a long time ago. Trouble was, she
sensed Ben Wyatt could easily rectify that if
she wasn't careful. She should have known
from his first phone call that he was very different from the others she'd dealt with.

Still, she silently decided, looking at him
was most definitely a feast for the eyes.

He was tall, probably around six foot two
or three. His dark emerald eyes looked as if
they could slice right through someone and
see all the things that person was trying to
hide. The black hair still maintained a stylish
cut but looked long overdue for another and
seemed to resist any efforts at taming. She
sensed the man was the same way. Lean, moving with the grace of a jungle cat. A dangerous
man. A very dangerous man.

Still, she reminded herself, she'd worked
with many dangerous men and come out
unscathed.

This man is different, the practical side of
her brain informed her. *He doesn't play by the
rules you learned so long ago. His showing up here
uninvited is proof of that.*

And I've changed. No reason why I can't take

what might be offered without a hitch, her hormones countered.

Right, and you'll return to L.A. next week to take up where you left off.

Cruel, brain, really cruel.

Then keep your brains on business and your glands on ice.

Nothing in Kelly's expression gave away the mental battle going on inside.

"Is there something wrong with the way Casey and I do business that the big boss has to step in?" she asked amiably, placing her hands, with the fingers laced, on the table in front of her.

"Not at all. I thought since I was in the area, I would take the time to meet the artist behind the clothing that does so well in my shops. As for Casey, there were complications and she had to take her maternity leave earlier than expected," he explained.

Her eyes displayed sincere concern. "Is she all right? There's nothing wrong with her baby, is there?"

"No, the doctor just feels she shouldn't continue her intense traveling and recommends rest. She claims she'll be back to work in six months. I told her not to worry, because there's always a position open for her," he replied. "Since one of her stops would be here to negotiate your next shipment to us, I thought I'd take care of it myself."

"Um, I love to negotiate," Kelly almost purred, making the usually dry rounds of business give-and-take sound downright sensuous.

"Then shall we discuss it over dinner tonight at the hotel?" he asked, wanting to hear that sexy purr again, and soon.

"Lunch, one o'clock tomorrow at my house," she said quickly, not giving him a reason as to why she couldn't meet with him that evening.

Ben knew better than to ask her for that reason. His business instincts told him she wanted to meet with him on her turf. Besides, the idea of an intimate lunch didn't sound all that bad to him. Not to mention the fact that he wasn't about to make any sudden moves around here. Good ol' Del, with his muscles piled upon muscles, looked as if he wanted the least excuse to turn Ben into oatmeal.

"I'll write out directions for you." Kelly quickly sketched a map on a piece of scrap paper and handed it to him. "I have a good one or two more hours' worth of book work here, so I'll see you tomorrow." She politely, but firmly, dismissed him as she returned to perusing the ledger in front of her.

"Tomorrow, then." He picked up his barely touched drink and stood up.

Under the cover of lowered lashes, Kelly watched Ben walk away, his loose-hipped gait forcing her to admire the lean muscles moving beneath the lightweight slacks. She only hoped she'd have herself under control by the time he showed up for lunch the next day. She silently damned her impulsive invitation to her house. Common sense suggested she should have met him in the hotel dining room instead. She sensed she'd be better off if she had a lot of people around her when she dealt with him.

Her eyes widened in surprise when she noticed him choose a table that would be sure to give him a clear view of her table . . . and her.

"I can still get rid of him, Kelly," Del rumbled, setting a fresh glass of diet cola in front of her.

"That's all right, Del. Thanks." She smiled up at him. "He'll get bored soon enough of our primitive ambience and head back to the hotel. I can't imagine this is his usual kind of hangout."

Kelly should have remembered a cardinal

rule of business: Never underestimate one's opponent. As she figured out the month's bills and deciphered Del's chicken scratches on the order lists, she felt Ben's gaze on her, unwavering. There was no threat, no overt leers or undressing of her with those gorgeous green eyes. Too bad. Those she could have easily ignored. But when he caught her eye and looked at her as if there was something very elemental between them, when she'd already convinced herself her attraction to him was nothing more than displaced hormones, she knew she had to watch herself or she could end up in a lot of trouble. She decided she would just wait him out. That was it. She'd just stay here until either he left or the tavern closed. She'd bet on the former.

Kelly soon learned she was wrong. Ben nursed two drinks the whole evening and didn't leave the tavern until just before it closed. The entire time he was there Kelly felt him watching her, probably dissecting her. While she wasn't about to let him know she was watching him, she did indulge in some visual dissection of her own. The man was good looking in a rugged way. The kind of man who belonged more on a sheep station than one who owned and ran a successful chain of boutiques found in the more luxurious resort hotels from Australia and New Zealand to Hawaii. When Del yelled out last call for drinks, Ben stood up, nodded in Kelly's direction, and left the tavern without a backward glance. Polite, sharp, and unnerving. She knew she'd have to watch her step with him tomorrow. Usually, she enjoyed her evenings at the Rusty Nail. Tonight, she was never so glad to leave and go home, where she hoped to regain her usual serenity.

Once she was safely inside her home she wandered through the darkened rooms, hoping the soft colors would soothe her the way they always did. She wasn't as lucky tonight. She still couldn't forget her first meeting with Ben Wyatt.

He's not for you, my girl, she silently told herself, opening drapes to reveal a lanai and the beach beyond. To accomplish all that he had he would have to be one of those driven types she used to know—and be— only too well. Look how profitable his shops had become since he opened the first one five years ago. And he did mention he was on his way to look over all his shops. Yep, he was type A all the way. Just the way she'd been once upon a time, and look where it got her. She stared out the window, watching the moonlight spill across the ocean in silvery bands.

Time in Treasure Cove had breathed new life into her body and mind. No more tension headaches, her ulcer had cleared up, and she now slept all night, no longer a victim of those horrible bouts of insomnia she had been prone to. She had even given up smoking, without having suffered too much nicotine withdrawal.

Kelly thought of calling Elaine for some old-fashioned girl talk. The time difference meant she wouldn't be waking her up. Except that Elaine knew her too well; after all, they'd been friends since high school. No, she would sense something was up and, using her best attorney's manner, would wheedle the information out of her. What could she say? That she'd met a man who turned her on? Elaine would stand up and cheer at that piece of news. No, better to stay away from the phone. What she needed now was peace. The kind of peace she'd found the moment she'd stepped onto the island almost a year ago.

Without thinking twice, Kelly headed for her workroom, where piles of T-shirts, cotton dresses, and tote bags awaited her brush. Fabric painting had turned out to be the best tranquilizer around, and had given her an excellent source of income too. She only hoped it would soothe her restless spirit tonight as well as it had in the past, when her fears of what the future held for her kept her moving constantly, too afraid to sit still for too long.

Unfortunately, she doubted it would work this time.

"Right on time, I see." It had taken hours for Kelly to come to this cool, calm, and collected manner that had once stood her in such good stead when she romanced prospective clients for her firm. A warm smile, but not too warm. Friendly, but not too friendly. Just a hint of a tease within a savvy businesswoman. A man's dream of the perfect woman.

"While island time is different from anyone else's idea of time, I tend to stick to what the clock says," Ben replied, stepping inside. He looked around at the light, airy feeling Kelly had given the room, with off-white walls accented by shades of peach, soft green, dusty rose, and pale blue in the furniture and artwork. He stared at the narrow bridge and at the small pond filled with brightly colored koi that it spanned. "I see you opted for a pond in your living room instead of an aquarium like everyone else."

"The pond was already built when I bought the house. The previous owner went in for overstatement when he had the house built," Kelly explained, leading him over the bridge. "I heard he actually wanted a shark tank, but his wife talked him out of it. Story is his second choice was piranha."

Ben chuckled as he looked down at the fish just under the water's surface. "Must have been a lawyer or stockbroker. It sounds like something one of them would want in his house."

"He just fancied himself an individualist who liked to have odd topics of conversation surrounding him." She gestured toward the lanai, which overlooked a private beach. A glass-topped table was covered with a variety of small bowls.

"How did you get lucky enough to be the owner?" Ben said, eyeing the varied food supplies with interest.

"He decided just because it was to be a getaway house didn't mean he would leave his computers and fax machine behind. The thing is, he didn't realize he'd have to build a climate-controlled room for them. In the end, he decided it wasn't worth the expense since he'd probably be here only a few weeks a year. Now, for lunch. What you see are the makings for a Mexican feast guaranteed to burn a good-sized hole in your stomach. We have spiced ground beef, guacamole, salsa, flour and corn tortillas, shredded cheese, tomatoes, onions." She pointed out the contents. "Would you like a beer?" She opened a small ice chest and extracted a bottle of Corona.

"What else would you have with Mexican food?" Ben sat down and accepted the icy bottle. He squeezed lime into it and drank deeply. Seeing that she didn't stand on ceremony, he helped himself to a little from each bowl and soon drank more beer to settle the inferno in his mouth. "Don't tell me—your cook's name is Consuela."

"No cook. I just enjoy Mexican food and am lucky enough that a friend is able to send me the basics every couple of months." She loaded beef into a curved taco shell and topped it with a little of everything.

Ben followed, piling a great deal of the hot salsa on top. "I have to admit that after your less than cordial greeting yesterday, I'm surprised you were willing to entertain me today."

Kelly looked up. "One of my rules is no

discussing business during a meal. When you called and asked to meet me, I said no. Then you showed up on my doorstep. I figured it was easier to just go ahead and get this over with, so you can get on with your travels and I can get back to my life."

His eyes gleamed with respect at her plain talk. "You don't believe in mincing words, do you?"

"I left the double-talk behind in L.A."

Ben knew he should have been concentrating on business instead of visualizing his nibbling that bit of guacamole off her lower lip. The pale yellow shorts and yellow and red floral tank top was appropriate for the tropical weather. It also showed off a slender figure he was appreciating more by the second. It was easy to tell she wasn't wearing a bra under the thin cotton. Her face was artfully made up, but still couldn't hide the ravages of a sleepless night. He hoped he was the reason for her restless hours, just as he'd paced his hotel suite most of the night because his sleep had been haunted by a woman's face. For a man who usually took things slow and easy and was rarely captivated by a woman so swiftly, he found himself on a rollercoaster ride, courtesy of a pair of cool caramel eyes that he wanted to see turn into the cloudy gaze of the passionate woman he sensed was hidden by this sharp-witted businesswoman.

"You don't wear your own creations?"

"Not when I'm eating Mexican food. I tend to be messy when I eat tacos." She looked up, and noticed he was staring at her rather than eating. "You don't like Mexican food? Is it too spicy for you?"

"No problem there. I like *everything* hot."

Kelly's eyes held his for several silent moments. It appeared the battle would be who would lower theirs first. By unspoken agreement, they returned to their food at the same time. Taking the hint, Ben concentrated on his meal, eating heartily and savoring every bite.

"After all the hotel food I've eaten the past couple of weeks, this is a wonderful change," he complimented. "As an unwanted guest, I didn't expect anything so elaborate. Thank you."

She warmed under his sincere praise. "I know what you mean about hotel food. After awhile, it all looks the same and you forget where you are. I think all the hotels use the same menus."

"Then you must have traveled a lot."

"I've done my share," she said cryptically.

Ben stroked the long neck of his beer bottle. "You're a very mysterious person."

"Oh?"

"Some of the people around here say you've been married, others feel you've always been single. Word has it you bought the Rusty Nail because you said you needed a tax loss, and yet you're using up a lot of black ink in your ledgers because business is better than ever— since, unlike the previous owner, you don't water the drinks and you make it a place the locals can relax in. You don't talk about your past and tend to freeze off anyone who tries to push past the barrier you've erected. You're the island mystery, and many enjoy keeping you that way. I gather they enjoy speculating about you and might even fear that the truth would ruin it all for their fertile minds."

Her face appeared carved from pale gold marble. "It appears you've been a busy man this morning, Mr. Wyatt. I thought you were here to talk business. My personal life is just that: personal."

He was unfazed by her cold tone. "I'm just trying to get to know you. There's nothing wrong with that, is there?"

"It depends on what you want to know. So,

tell me about yourself." She sat back, keeping the smirk off her face, but Ben knew it was lying beneath the surface. She seemed to enjoy turning the tables on him.

"I'm thirty-six, never been married because I haven't found a woman who's fascinated me enough for me to want to take the plunge. I'm one of three boys, my father is the driving force behind a large accounting firm in Sydney, I've had all the requisite childhood diseases, and right now, there's no one special in my life." He spoke each word in a deliberate tone meant to keep her gaze on him. "I also have a healthy imagination that right now sees the two of us in a darkened bedroom making love as if the world could end at any moment."

TWO

"You're right, Mr. Wyatt. You do have a very healthy imagination." Kelly blessed her business background for having provided her with the common sense to sit there looking as if he'd said nothing more innocuous than "Lovely weather, isn't it?" Especially when she'd felt all the air leave her body as he'd painted his mental picture. The way he was looking at her, she wouldn't be surprised if he could see all the way through her top to the tiny mole dotting the top of her right breast. "Perhaps you should try writing a book."

Ben's gaze dropped for a micro-second to the puckered nipples pressing against the soft cotton of her top, then lifted to silently tell her she wasn't as composed as she pretended to be.

"Ocean breezes are generally cool in the afternoons."

His smile was slow and devastating, especially to a woman who hadn't made love in almost two years. Once she had learned the truth about Michael's bed-hopping, she'd locked him out of the bedroom and out of her life.

"You're very quick with the words, Kelly," he said softly. "I like that in a woman. It shows she isn't afraid to prove she has a brain along with a lovely face." He sat back in his chair, his arm draped across the top, his fingertips rubbing reflectively across his mouth. The fact that he was able to draw her gaze to that motion wasn't lost on him.

Kelly refused to consider what she might be feeling. Ben wasn't movie-star handsome, nor did he have the toothpaste smile or charm that could sweep most women into bed. A tiny scar by the lower corner of his left eye added to the masculine appeal. A turquoise cotton shirt and stone-colored cotton shorts, along with bare feet in battered deck shoes, told her he was a man who didn't worry about outward appearances. What she knew about his business told her he always got what he wanted. And right now, he wanted her.

"I'm not part of the deal, Mr. Wyatt." Her gentle tone was meant to be a definite turnoff.

He frowned, surprised she'd looked at it that way. "This is separate from our business dealings, Kelly. You can say all you want, but I can see an attraction beginning between us. I know it, and if you'd care to look at the truth, you'd admit it too."

"I went through a nasty divorce about a year ago, and—even if I were interested, which I'm not—I don't think I'm ready for someone like you," she said bluntly.

He tucked the piece of information away in his memory bank. "You won't know until you try."

Kelly carefully placed her napkin on the table and stood up. "I think this would be a good time for you to see what you pay so much money for."

He cocked an eyebrow. "Running away?"

"Not at all. Just regrouping my forces."

Ben smiled. He didn't mind walking behind Kelly one bit. Not when the view was just as enticing as it was from the front. He usually wasn't the type to come on so heavy to a woman, but something about Kelly told him that if he didn't corral her soon he could lose out on something very special. Something he'd been looking for for a long time.

Kelly led the way down a narrow hallway. "This was to have been the previous owner's office. I tore out the walls and put in floor-to-ceiling windows so I wouldn't feel closed in." She pushed open the door and stepped back so Ben could enter first.

Ben always classified a creative mind two ways: obsessively neat and obsessively sloppy. Kelly turned out to be a little of each.

Shelves holding various items of clothing covered the walls, with neatly typed labels tacked to the shelves identifying items and sizes. Blank canvas tote bags were stacked against one wall and ones already painted were carefully hung on wall pegs. Another set of shelves held multicolored bottles of fabric paints and dyes.

He studied each bag, noticing the differences in scenes. It was these little touches that always identified Kelly's work to him.

"Lovely," he murmured, touching one bag with his fingers.

Kelly studied the same bag. She still remembered the day she'd watched children playing at the water's edge, the way they'd laughed as the water swirled around their ankles, how they'd jumped out of its way. She had re-created the scene on the side of a large tote bag.

"The larger bags are more popular now because people like to conserve paper when they're shopping," she explained. "And that scene required a larger bag."

Ben spun around. "Why isn't this work shown on an artist's canvas in an art gallery? You have a remarkable talent. I would hate losing such a gifted fabric artist, but what you do is impressive."

She shrugged, uneasy under his praise and grateful he appeared to have forgotten their earlier, more personal conversation. "I first grew interested in painting in high school. Unfortunately, I was told my talent was mediocre, at best. When I decided to return to it, to see if there was anything there, I quickly learned I wasn't mediocre—I was downright terrible." She smiled wryly. "I later discovered fabric painting and got the hang of it after throwing out a lot of my mistakes. My neighbor told people I had the most colorful trash on the island."

Ben moved on to look at painted silky cotton T-shirts and several cotton sundresses with pastel floral designs decorating either their hemlines or their straps and bodices. No two items were alike.

"My mother has two of your dresses, several T-shirts, and one of your bags," he murmured, examining the delicate brush lines of dark purple irises painted along the hem of a pale lilac cotton dress. "She demands to see your work before they're sent out to the shops, so she can have first choice."

Kelly smiled. "I'm glad to have such a devoted fan. Walking advertisements are always the best."

"She's that, all right." Ben turned to face her. "Are you going to hold me up for more money now that I've shown such a sincere appreciation for your work?"

"I left the heavy-duty wheeling and dealing in my past, but I will give you a run for your money." She grinned.

He winced. "Fine. Your products won't wear as well as others, the brush strokes are uneven, and your designs are so unique we have to put a higher than usual price on them, so we see very little profit in the end."

"With proper care, my designs wear very well. The brush strokes are perfect, and many women believe the higher the price the better the product. If you don't want them, David

Chew has been asking me about carrying my designs in his stores." She leaned against her worktable, looking entirely at ease now that she had thrown the ball into his court.

He made a face as he recognized the name of his chief competitor. "His stores have horrible lighting, are in lousy locations, and he couldn't give you the floor space I do."

"He's promised to throw in his mother's recipe for shrimp in lobster sauce as a bonus."

"The way my mother cooks, you wouldn't want any of her recipes, except to burn them. I'll give you an extra one and a half percent for each item sold."

"Six."

"Two and three quarters."

"Five and a half."

Ben grinned. This was a part of business he enjoyed, and bargaining with a desirable woman gave it a new edge. "Four and a quarter."

Kelly didn't answer right away. "Five and a quarter and that's the lowest I'll go."

"Four and three quarters and feel lucky you got it, because you're destroying any hope I had of making a profit."

She concentrated on the tiny scar. "Split the difference and go for five?"

Ben held out his hand. "Done. Just as long

as dinner tonight at the hotel is thrown in. Considering the obscene amount of money I'll be paying you, I'll allow you to pick up the check."

"Considering I lowered my price to where I'm going to barely break even, *you* can pick up the check."

"Then we have a done deal," he said. She straightened up and grasped his hand. From the first second of contact, she felt the heat tingle all the way up her arm. His open shirt revealed a tuft of dark, curling hair that practically screamed an invitation to her fingers to comb. She silently ordered her hormones to play dead. She should have issued an order to Ben as well.

"*Now* we'll have a done deal," he murmured, slowing pulling her into his arms until she was nestled against him.

Kelly knew she was in trouble the moment his mouth covered hers. His tongue didn't request entrance into the dark cavern of her mouth; it demanded it. And she was powerless to resist. His hands splayed against her bare skin, burning an imprint as they stroked their way from the soft skin of her nape to the rolled-cloth edge of her top.

Kelly couldn't breathe, because there was

no air. There was only a vacuum in which no one else but the two of them existed. Part of her wanted nothing more than to crawl inside this man and discover everything he had to offer. Judging from the way he kissed, it was a great deal. Not content to be a passive partner, she ran her tongue along the slightly serrated edge of his teeth and moaned deep in her throat when his teeth closed lightly on the tip and drew it deeper into his mouth.

This was not the way she usually closed a business deal! But the things he was doing to her were so delicious, so necessary to a woman who'd banished affection from her life a long time ago, that she couldn't have stopped herself if she tried.

"Kelly," he whispered, pushing her tank top up so his fingers could spread out over the soft skin of her abdomen, where they rested below her breasts. "Believe me, I don't go for instant gratification, but there's something between us. Something neither of us can fight."

She shook her head violently. It took every ounce of willpower in her body, but she was finally able to step back and push him away from her.

"Mr. Wyatt," she gasped. She knew her breathing was labored, her face flushed, and her body too overheated to think straight. "I don't believe I've ever sealed a business deal in this manner, but then I've never met a man like you before either."

His face was sharply etched with his desire. He stood before her, uncaring that she was seeing him in his aroused state, a state that made it difficult for her to focus on his face rather than . . . She pulled in a deep trembling breath as she forced her eyes back upward to his face.

"I think you should leave."

Ben opened his mouth, fully prepared to argue—until he saw the tension etched so deeply in her face. Was she that unnerved about what was starting to happen between them? He was feeling more than just a lust that could be easily settled by a few hours between the sheets. Why wasn't she willing to at least give him a chance?

Kelly turned away and braced her hands on the worktable. She looked so vulnerable, Ben's heart ached for her.

"This is not a good idea," she said in a low voice.

"You told me you're not married, and I doubt you're running from the law. There's nothing to stop us from the inevitable."

She winced. *Oh sure, nothing except my so-called good sense.* "Since we've settled our transaction, I don't see any reason for you to stay."

He stepped forward. He wanted to put his arms around her and demand she tell him what was bothering her so much, but although he didn't know her well, he sensed she wouldn't appreciate any more moves on his part.

"I'll meet you in front of the hotel dining room at seven." He also sensed an offer to pick her up wouldn't be accepted.

Kelly said nothing. Ben took that as a good sign. She might not have said yes, she'd be there, but she didn't say no either. She threw him out instead. Without saying another word, he left her alone. He knew when to retreat.

Kelly didn't hear him leave the room, but she could sense it. She soon heard the soft snick of the front door closing. She stared out the floor-to-ceiling window at the picture-postcard view of the beach. She vaguely wondered where she might end up were she to just dive into the waves and start swimming. With her luck it would be Australia.

She used to have incredible timing. Always one step ahead of the competition. She could forecast changes before they happened. There were times she kept clients from losing hundreds of thousands of dollars, if not millions. So where was that sense of magic timing when she met Michael? Why hadn't she guessed what kind of sleaze his surface charm hid? she asked herself, pounding the table with her fist. And why did she have to just meet the sexiest, most fascinating man that she didn't dare have anything to do with? She turned her head, gazing at her phone. The temptation to call Elaine reared its head again. She already knew what her friend would say. "Go for it. Time is short. Take what you can get."

The idea sounded wonderful. Kelly had to admit she missed a man's arms around her, and when Ben kissed her she visualized them lying in bed together. But she also knew she couldn't go through with it. She didn't want to take the chance of falling in love with the same kind of businessman her father was.

A mental picture of her father filled her mind. Laughing, robust. Ross Andrews had been known as a true wheeler-dealer in his day. There were no social functions, only opportunities to make new business contacts. She was certain he'd coined the term "power lunch." And because he worked twenty hours a day building a business empire, he died of a heart attack just after his forty-second birthday.

The doctors said he'd overdone it. They talked about clogged arteries, high blood pressure, ulcers. And Kelly and her mother were left to pick up the pieces of a rapidly crumbling empire, minus its dynamic leader. Kelly had vowed she'd never allow that to happen to her husband, so she'd married a devil-may-care actor—and *she* became the go-getter. Oh yes, she was her father's daughter, showing her background by attending school during the summer so she could graduate with her master's degree two years early. By the time she was twenty-eight, she was nursing a bleeding ulcer, battling high blood pressure, and couldn't sleep more than a few hours a night. But she'd been smart enough to get out before she shared her father's fate. And she'd be damned if she'd allow herself to hook up with a man who was running in that same fast lane—a man like Ben Wyatt.

Ben worried she wouldn't show up. Feeling like a teenager on his first date, he'd left his suite a half hour early. He wasted time in the hotel bar sipping a bourbon and soda he didn't want and watched vacationers compare notes regarding other resorts and their amenities while imbibing colorful drinks. He smiled as he saw the many paper umbrellas and skewers of pineapple decorating the colorful drinks. It appeared even that made him think about Kelly. He kept glancing at his watch, waiting for the moment he could safely leave the bar and head for the dining room entrance. If several women flashed him inviting smiles as he walked by, he didn't notice. He was too busy remembering the woman he'd held in his arms that afternoon and realizing how much he wanted to hold her again.

She shouldn't have come. The moment Kelly entered the hotel's open-air lobby she told herself to just march right back out again. Then she saw Ben standing in front of the dining room entrance and all idea of resistance fled.

"I hope I haven't kept you waiting long."

He looked her over, observing the honey-colored hair tumbling down her back in loose curls and the cream-colored silk halter dress with a handkerchief hem that fluttered around her calves. Soft apricot and pale blue flowers decorated the scooped neckline and diamond-point hemline. Her only jewelry were coral earrings that dangled against her neck.

"Very lovely. Some of your own work?"

He nodded toward her dress, inhaling the soft fragrance that drifted off her skin.

She nodded. "One of my better attempts at painting on silk. I don't do it very often because mistakes can turn out to be very costly."

"You succeeded beautifully." He held out his arm. "Shall we go in?"

They were guided to a table overlooking the hotel gardens, where brilliant-colored parrots and macaws now dozed amid the tiki-torch-lit darkness. The view was lost on them, since they couldn't stop looking at each other.

Ben insisted on ordering champagne. "To toast our new contract. I talked to my office when I got back and the paperwork will be out to you in a couple of days."

Kelly's lips curved. "You don't waste any time, do you?"

"Not when it's important." His eyes glittered. It was apparent neither of them was talking about business. "Although, if I'd been concentrating more on our negotiations than on your legs, I would have insisted on longer terms."

She shook her head. "I prefer short-term arrangements. I never know when my creativity will run out."

"After what I saw today, I sincerely doubt that will happen."

After the champagne was poured and tasted, they lifted their glasses.

"To South Seas Boutiques. May they always present you with a huge profit margin," Kelly announced.

"And to the loveliest woman I've met in a long time, and one I hope to continue a long-running business relationship with," he countered.

"I should have stuck to six per cent."

His grin did strange things to Kelly's nervous system. "I would have given it to you."

"After that statement, poor Casey won't know what hit her when she and I negotiate my next contract."

Ben's gaze bored into her face. "You can try all you want, Kelly, but I'm not going away. If anything, you'll see more of me than you probably hoped for."

She licked her lips. It wasn't difficult to take that statement two ways. "Ben, you are a very attractive man and, yes, I sense there could be something growing between us, but there's a reason behind my not wanting to get involved with anyone. As it is, you'll be flying out of here tomorrow, and I was nev-

er one for one-night stands," she said flat-
ly.

"I might be flying out of here tomorrow,
but I'll be back," he stated.

"I can't imagine you'd go to so much trouble for one fabric artist." She wasn't sure she
liked the expression in his eyes. He had something up his sleeve.

He reached across the table and took her
hand, lacing his fingers between hers. "You're
right, I wouldn't, but I signed the paperwork
today to open a boutique here in the hotel. I'll
be personally overseeing the setup."

Kelly wasn't certain, but she thought her
heart might have momentarily stopped.

Ben looked down at their entwined fingers.
"I already know you aren't repulsed by me."

She resisted the urge to fan her face.
Didn't they believe in air-conditioning here?
she wondered. "I doubt any red-blooded woman would be."

He lifted his eyes. "Then will you give it
a chance? Us a chance? Believe me, Kelly, I've
never come on this strong to a woman before.
It's bowled me over just as much as it has you.
I won't ask you for more than you can give, so
will you at least give it a try?" he asked. "We
can have harmless picnics on the beach, walks,

maybe take in a movie in the hotel theater.
What do you say?"

Say no, her practical side ordered. *This is
not good, Kelly. He's a wheeler-dealer like Dad
was. Look how fast he worked up a contract to open
a boutique here? Doesn't that tell you something
about the man? So what if he has a fit-looking
body? Dad did too. It didn't save his life.*

Say yes! her hormones practically screamed
in her mind. *This man is not Michael or your dad.
He clearly desires you the same way you want him.
And he doesn't look like the kind of man to die in
bed. Admit it, Kelly: You want to jump his bones.
So go for it!*

"What can I say?" she whispered.

" 'Yes' would be a nice word to start with,"
he murmured, lifting the back of her hand to
his lips. He didn't merely kiss her hand, he
nibbled on it as if it were a delicate appetizer.

Kelly stifled the sigh welling up in her
throat. "I've been a sucker for an Australian
accent since the first time I heard Mel Gibson
speak."

Her fate was sealed when she read delight
in his gaze, and not triumph. He didn't view
her assent as winning the first phase of a game,
the way Michael would have. Michael always
enjoyed playing sexual games. That was when

she knew making love with Ben would be just what he said: incredible.

She remembered little of the meal she ate or what they talked about. When Ben suggested a walk on the beach she could only nod her head in agreement while Ben signed the check.

Kelly stopped at the edge of the sand to slip off her sandals, then dangled them from her hand. Ben kept the other hand firmly warmed by his grip.

"This is what paradise is all about," he said huskily, looking up at a full moon that sent silvery sparkles through the air and iridescent streamers across the water.

"It is a world unto itself," she agreed as they walked through the still-warm sand. She forced herself not to tense up at the idea of his kissing her again. As if she'd remain tense for long, considering the way he kissed! She'd discovered that afternoon just what it meant to melt in a man's arms. Now she found herself wanting to see if that electric jolt would happen again. She hated herself for wanting it to.

They walked down the beach, their hips bumping together companionably as Ben spoke of impersonal topics: the latest novel he'd read, the movie he'd seen a few weeks ago, his hopes for the new boutique. He asked Kelly her opinion about the shop. And all the time she was screaming inside, waiting for him to make his move.

Ben glanced down at his watch. "If you don't mind, we probably should return to the hotel. I have an early flight to catch."

Here it comes, she thought. *The oh-so-casual "Would you care to come up to my room for a drink?" ploy.* She resisted the urge to smirk.

"All right."

Even on the way back to the bright hotel lights, Ben was nothing more than the proper companion. A business associate, nothing more. He offered Kelly his arm when she brushed the sand off her feet and slipped her sandals back on, then guided her into the hotel lobby.

"I'm very glad we had this time to get to know each other," he told her.

She was still geared up for that invitation. Surely he wouldn't kiss her here? The way he kissed, it would definitely attract a lot of attention. "Same here."

It wasn't until Ben stopped that Kelly realized they were standing by the hotel entrance, instead of the elevators.

"If I can arrange my schedule accordingly, I should be back in a week or so. Until then." He held out his hand and a stunned Kelly could only grasp it for a very businesslike handshake. Ben presented her with the kind of smile that jolted her right down to her toes, and with a nod of the head he left her.

Kelly watched Ben stride toward the elevators. Hers weren't the only female eyes watching him, and she hated herself for standing there and watching him like a lovesick calf. And she hated him for entering the elevator car without turning around.

"You can come back next week, Ben Wyatt. Just don't expect to find me welcoming you with open arms," she muttered, walking out of the hotel before she did something foolish. Such as storm Ben's room and have her wicked way with him.

THREE

"Make my day. Please, tell me you have a man in your life. And that he's absolutely gorgeous and has an equally gorgeous brother with scads of money he wants to spend on li'l ole' me."

Kelly laughed as she adjusted the telephone receiver more comfortably against her ear.

"Elaine, don't you have enough going on in your life without worrying about mine? Besides, I don't think he's your type."

Her friend and attorney gave a shriek that easily carried across the thousands of miles of ocean. "I knew it! Tell all. Who is he? Gorgeous, I'm sure. Is he great in bed? Give me a break, Kelly! I want all the details!"

"Get a life, Elaine!" she laughed, then her laughter abruptly stilled as Ben came to mind.

"Available men aren't exactly plentiful out here. Besides, I want to hear what's going on out there."

"Michael is still threatening to sue you for his dental bills and the trauma that losing his caps caused him, and his sleaze of an attorney insists you belong in jail for that black eye you gave him. The fact that you decked them on the courthouse steps where it was caught on film for the six and eleven o'clock news didn't help. Michael's threatening to demand a good piece of your holdings. I told him that when you dissolved the firm's partnership with Gordon your half of the proceeds paid all the bills and he should be happy that he got the house, the cars, and the cat." Her tone told Kelly just how much she hated talking to Kelly's ex-husband.

"Although it looks like he's going to be punished soon enough." Elaine went on. "Rumor has it he's going to develop some disfiguring disease and be written out of the show. I also heard he consulted a Beverly Hills plastic surgeon. Poor boy must have imagined a tiny line somewhere and is afraid it will affect his so-called career. After all, he is only known for taking his shirt off at opportune times, those steamy looks he gives the women, and his so-called engaging smiles. Nothing has ever been said about his having any talent."

"Maybe he woke up one morning and found a zit on the end of his nose," Kelly said, looking at the note pad she'd been doodling on while Elaine spoke. A fairly accurate caricature of Michael with a raging case of acne looked up at her. She smiled. "Perhaps I should call the show's writers and offer some ideas."

"Oh, Kel, I miss you!" Elaine wailed. "There's no one who understands me the way you do. I miss our weekly lunches where we bitch about anything that's bothering us."

"I thought Ron would keep you so busy you wouldn't have time to miss me."

"He turned forty and found an eighteen-year-old bimbo to make him feel young again."

"Oh, Elaine," Kelly sympathized. "Still, maybe it's for the best. He always seemed to be too interested in his dental practice, to the exclusion of anything else. Have you met anyone new?" She devoutly hoped the question would keep her friend's mind off Kelly's lack of a sex life.

Elaine went on about the few times she'd gone out and the disasters each date had turned out to be.

"If only you'd come back."

"I can't," Kelly said quietly, but firmly.

"Because you're afraid you'll get caught up in that same old rat race?" Elaine was nothing if not intuitive. "You can't get caught up if you don't want to."

"It would be too easy to fall back into my old ways. All it would take is running into an old colleague or client and I'd soon be talking business and subscribing to the *Wall Street Journal* and *Fortune* magazine again," Kelly sighed. "Here, there's no pressure; no desire to run at the head of the pack. I can eat spicy food without swallowing half a bottle of Maalox afterward, and jangled nerves that are running strictly on caffeine are a thing of the past. I can actually sleep all night. I'm happy here, El."

"I'm glad for that," Elaine said sincerely. "Even if I do miss you like hell. Maybe I should toss my practice out the window and take off for an island too."

"You might like it," Kelly said lightly.

"Yes, but I've got all those wonderful clothes you left me. While so many others figured we hardheaded businesswomen should only wear gray flannel and subtle stripes, you were wowing them in lipstick-red raw-silk dresses and teal wool suits that I'm enjoying to no end. I'm just glad we wear the same size shoe, so I could indulge in all those matching shoes and handbags too," she laughed. "And then there's that fuchsia suit with the matching accessories that I very happily took off your hands."

Kelly swallowed a tiny sigh. She remembered that suit very well. The vibrant color always gave her a much-needed lift. It had been a designer original, very expensive, and she considered it worth every penny. She hated giving that one up, but she didn't want to take any reminders of her past life with her. She came back down to earth as her friend's words began to sink in.

"I only wish I knew how it happened," Elaine went on. "One minute I'm eating dinner, the next this burgundy sauce is all over the jacket! The cleaners doubt they'll be able to get the stain out."

Kelly's fingers tightened around her pencil until the wood cylinder snapped. "I can imagine it upset you."

"Upset me? All I could think about was you! I mean, Kelly, you practically worshiped that suit! You considered it your good-luck charm. I feel as if I should buy it a coffin and bury it at Forest Lawn!"

Kelly gritted her teeth. "No, it was just another suit, and it's yours now," she forced herself to say. "Look, El, I've got to run. You take care and I'll send you those sweatshirts with some new designs."

"Oh, great! Everyone wants to know where I get them, but I never let on. Take care, sweetie."

Kelly forced herself to carefully lower the receiver into the cradle. "My fuchsia suit," she said between clenched teeth. "I wore that suit when I snapped up the Garibaldi account! I searched all over Southern California for shoes to match that suit, then ended up having a pair specially made when I went to Italy. Burgundy sauce!" she practically screamed. When the phone rang she snatched it up before the first ring had barely finished. "What?" she fairly snarled into the receiver.

"Gotcha."

"Elaine, I hate you!"

"Just be grateful nothing happened to the suit," she chuckled. "Now that I've got you thinking about something other than the lack of men on that island, I'll ring off."

"If you were here I'd push you into the nearest volcano!"

"I don't think so. One, there aren't any volcanoes on that island; you told me so yourself. Two, they usually require virgins."

When Kelly hung up the second time, she realized Elaine had accomplished one thing. Her little joke had gotten Kelly to forget all about Ben. For a whole two minutes.

"He's back."

Kelly slowly opened her eyes and looked up. "Who?"

The dark haired woman gave her a knowing look as she sat on the chaise longue next to the one a bikini-clad Kelly reclined on as she relaxed in the early-morning sun. "You know very well who." Her slight French accent gave her speech a musical lilt.

"Lili, word games don't become you," Kelly chided, stretching her arms over her head. After working through most of the night on several new designs, she'd opted for a short nap on the terrace instead of retreating to the dark haven of her bedroom. Lately, beds sent her thoughts skittering in Ben's direction, and that was not the direction she wanted them going in!

Lili Martine was the owner of a gift and jewellry shop in town that did a brisk business, thanks to her knack of knowing what the customer wanted. She and her husband, who ran a deep-sea fishing charter service, along with their four children, lived down the beach from Kelly.

"I hate people who won't look their age even when they reach eighty," Kelly muttered, slipping her dark glasses back on.

"And I've told you to be happy I admitted my age is over forty," the older woman chided in her musical accent.

"Talk about depressing. You're over forty, you don't look over thirty, and you have more energy than a twenty-year-old. I hate people like you."

Lili waved a well-manicured finger at her. "Do not try to evade me, *cherie*. We have a man to discuss, which is much more important than any talk of age."

Kelly faked a broad yawn. "I'm not evading anything."

"Yes you are, and I won't allow it. Ben Wyatt is a very good-looking man, very virile," Lili announced. "And he's perfect for you."

Kelly rolled her eyes. "He's a business colleague."

"Does that have to stop him from becoming your lover?"

By now, Kelly knew, she should be used

to her friend's frank talk, but that was easier said than done when Lili's primary goal in life seemed to be to pair Kelly with a man. "Maybe I don't want a lover!" she protested.

"Of course you do," Lili insisted. "A woman is not complete without a man. Lovemaking is very beneficial. It keeps a woman young."

Kelly eyed her speculatively. "I admit that if good sex could make me look like you I'd give it a try, but without a written guarantee on its benefits I'm not going to take any chances."

Lili laughed throatily as she stood up. She paused long enough to pat Kelly's hand. "We all want you to be happy, Kelly. And we feel Ben Wyatt is the man to do it. Isn't it wonderful he'll be here for a while to personally set up his new boutique? I understand he's always left that up to others before. He must have found something very fascinating here to want to stay." She shot Kelly a knowing look.

Kelly threw up her hands. "What is going on? Are all of you taking bets on my love life?"

"Hm, a lottery might make it more interesting. Don't forget that we're having our party tomorrow evening. Come early." With a wiggle of fingers, Lili headed for the beach.

"Maybe I'll give up parties!" Kelly called after her.

"No, you won't. Ours are too much fun! I will see you tomorrow night." She turned around to walk backward. "And do not be late'"

Kelly should have known that Lili would be only the first to enjoy giving her the news of Ben's return. Several people she knew stopped her on her way to the Rusty Nail early that evening to tell her Ben had checked into the hotel. Even Del glumly informed her, "That guy with the accent is back." She sat at her usual table and covertly watched the entrance. Many came and went, but not the man she was looking for. She only hoped her disappointment didn't show, and hated herself for even feeling it.

When she went home, she sought solace the best way she knew how—swimming until her arms ached and her skin tingled from her exertion.

Since privacy was the main reason Kelly had bought the house, she was comfortable swimming in the nude, especially late at night. As she walked from her house and into the warm water, she didn't see the tall figure watching her from the rise above. Nor did she hear his swift indrawn breath when the moonlight gilded her naked body. But she sensed his presence. Just before she reached the water's edge, she turned around and caught her observer's gaze. Then she turned and walked farther into the water. He remained where he was, watching her swim, listening to the soft sounds of her body slicing through the water.

The entire time Kelly swam, she felt his gaze on her. She took in a deep breath and dove under, but she couldn't hide from him. Finally, she headed for the shore and walked out of the water, feeling the cool water stream down her body. When she reached her towel, she found him waiting for her.

"I only meant to stop by and say hello," Ben said quietly, handing her the towel.

She accepted it and began drying off her body. If she was embarrassed at standing there naked while he was fully clothed, she didn't show it.

"Then hello." She lifted her hand to pull the clip holding her hair secure on top of her head, but Ben stayed her hand. Holding her gaze captive, he loosened the clip and watched her hair tumble down around her shoulders in honeyed waves.

"All the time I was gone I could only think

of you. Not just how much I wanted you, but all I wanted to learn about you. Your favorite books, movies, colors, foods, what you think about everything in general." He curled a strand of hair around his fingers, fascinated by the way the moonlight shone along the waves. "I was going to prove to you what a gentleman I can be by not showing up until breakfast time, but I couldn't stay away that long. I needed to see you, to see if my dreams were true."

Her throat ached. "Were they?"

His eyes returned to hers. "Yes."

Kelly licked her lips. "Would you care to stay for breakfast?"

Relief at her not telling him to go away flickered across his face. "What time do you want me back?"

She lifted her face as she whispered the words she couldn't believe she was saying, even as she realized she had no choice but to voice them. "Who says you have to come back?"

Ben swore under his breath. Whether it was a curse or a prayer, Kelly wasn't certain. He didn't waste any more time as he stepped forward and took her in his arms, inching her face to his. His kiss was that of a man hungry for a woman he'd dreamed about for the past ten days, his need that of a man bent on proving he wasn't still dreaming.

Her mouth opened readily under his probing tongue as he gathered her up against his body.

"I'll get you wet," she murmured in weak protest when he finally let her come up for air.

He picked her up in his arms. "Then I'll just have to take everything off so they can dry, won't I?" He carried her up the beach to the glass sliding door that led to her bedroom and pushed it open with his elbow.

"We could be making a very big mistake," Kelly told him, even as her arms around his neck tightened.

He walked inside and carefully set her on her feet. He rested his hands on the curve of her waist. "If you want me to leave, I will."

She studied his face in the shifting shadows the moon cast in the room, and read so much in his features. She sensed he was a man of his word. She only needed to say one word and he would leave and never bother her again if she didn't want him to. She also thought about the last ten days, and how lonely she'd felt—a loneliness that had begun before then, but that had intensified since she'd met him.

"Stay."

Only Ben knew how difficult it was for Kelly to say that one word. Only Ben could appreciate it for what it was.

He dipped his head and ran his open mouth over the taut skin of her throat before settling over the pulse point, which he nipped lightly, then soothed with his tongue. Her machine gun pulse rate wasn't lost on him as he continued his tiny nips along her collarbone before moving upward.

Kelly could only close her eyes, hang on to his shoulders, and hope her legs didn't give out.

"Ben!" she keened.

"I don't intend to rush this, Kelly," he told her in his husky voice, now rough with desire. "We've got all night to learn about each other, although I doubt that will be enough time for me."

She began tearing at his shirt, until he stepped back long enough to pull it over his head and unzip his shorts, then step out of them. He wore no underwear, so there was no hiding his arousal from her equally hungry eyes. Her tongue appeared to moisten her lips. Ben lowered his head and gently grasped her tongue between his teeth, grazing the damp surface. But light touches and teasing kisses soon weren't enough. Not after they'd dreamed about each other for so long.

Kelly ran her hands over Ben's chest, tangling her fingers in the crisp mat of hair that arrowed down to his waist and then resumed below, where it grew thick and coarse again. She wrapped her fingers around him, smiling at the hiss of air escaping between his teeth as she learned the motions that drove him wild; she leaned forward to touch the tip of her tongue to his nipple, feeling it swiftly turn into a copper nub under her ministrations. She would have been content tasting and touching him all over, but Ben had other ideas. Muttering that he was rapidly losing his sanity, he pushed her back onto the bed and followed her down.

Before Kelly could breathe a word, Ben had one leg curved around her calves as he covered her breast with his hand, softly rotating his hand against the swelling flesh and occasionally ducking his head to draw the nipple deep into his mouth. Kelly cried out as the suckling motion reached all the way into the deepest part of her body. She arched up under his touch and grabbed hold of his shoulders.

"You taste like the sea," he muttered

hoarsely, moving his head to give her other breast the same loving attention while one hand traveled downward to rest briefly against her concave belly before moving farther down to the nest of honey-colored curls. He easily found her moist warmth as his thumb and forefinger rubbed the tiny nub between them, sending shock waves throughout her body.

Kelly cried out as her body jerked in reaction. She had no idea that one man, with just the touch of his fingertips, could make such a difference. Heat radiated everywhere as Ben's fingers performed magic on her body.

"Not without you!" she cried, trying to lower his body to hers. Already light splintered around her and she felt as if time was passing her by. "Not without you!"

He moved over her until his hips rested intimately against hers. His arousal gently probed her, insuring that she was ready for him. His first thrust was strong and sure and Kelly exploded; before she could come down, Ben's rhythmic thrusts sent her spiraling again. Her voice came out high-pitched, crying for something she couldn't understand, and before she could regain her sanity she began to shatter once more, this time with Ben joining her. She thought she heard him shouting her name, but she had no idea because for a bare second blackness descended on her and she had no awareness of the outside world. Deep down, she knew that what she had just shared with Ben was something so special that she would never know its equal with anyone else. She wasn't sure whether to feel happiness or sorrow. At that moment, she didn't care, because all that mattered was the man holding her in his arms as if she were the most precious of china.

Kelly didn't want to open her eyes. Opening her eyes meant returning to reality, and after the night she'd just had she feared reality might never be the same.

Probably because lying in her own bed didn't feel the same. Probably because the very air around her didn't feel the same. The lightweight drapes moved with the morning breeze, generating a stronger than usual air current that carried on it the faint sounds of children's voices.

She tried to move, but her muscles protested, as did the arm flung across her middle. She turned her head and found Ben's head resting on her pillow, his eyes closed, cheeks and chin shadowed with morning beard. For an instant he reminded her of a sleeping boy, but she well knew this was no boy. This was a man who knew just how to get a response from a woman. Her nerve endings tingled with remembrance.

She'd lost track of the times they'd come together in the darkness. She knew only that each time had been better than the last, if that was possible.

Well, you've had your one-night stand with the guy, her hormones jeered. *Are you satisfied?*

Not for the next hundred years! All she had to do was look at him and she wanted him all over again.

As if sensing her gaze, he opened his eyes and offered a sleepy smile. His arm tightened around her as it drew her toward him for a leisurely kiss that easily could have ignited more if Kelly hadn't pulled back.

"The sun is up," she said huskily, already hating herself for offering such a ridiculous excuse.

"We could always close the drapes," he murmured, nuzzling her neck. "You're a very potent drug, Kelly. The more I have, the more I want."

She had to put some distance between them while she still could. She wiggled out of his arms and climbed out of bed, then headed for the closet and pulled out a robe.

Ben remained on his side, braced up on his elbow. The sheets slid down past his waist, but he appeared not to notice or care.

"The sunlight makes you modest?"

Kelly pressed her fingertips against her forehead in a vain attempt to think rationally. "I'd like to blame it on moon madness or the tropical air or something equally inane, but I can't," she said, stumbling over her words.

His brows pulled together in a frown. "What exactly are you trying to say, Kelly? You can't lie and say it wasn't enjoyable. I know better."

She flushed. Yes, Ben certainly did know, because she had told him, and showed him, enough times.

"I thought I could handle a one-night stand, but I should have known better. It just isn't my style."

He straightened up further. "And you think it's mine? I outgrew that need years ago! I thought what we shared was something very special."

"It was!" she insisted, hoping tears wouldn't follow. She knew she wouldn't be able to handle it if she started to cry. "We don't live even remotely close to each other! You're here for only a short time and then you'll be off doing what you do best: running your business. I told myself that an affair with you would be fine, but now I'm not so sure, and I'd rather you know that now instead of later!" She waved her hands as words failed. Muttering a curse under her breath, she headed for the bathroom, certain that only a long, hot shower would help her clear her thoughts.

She turned on the water and stepped into the cubicle, reaching for the special sea-weed soap wrapped in a loofah that she enjoyed so much. Here, with the water streaming over her face, she didn't care if she cried, because no one would know.

She almost screamed when the shower door opened and a dark-visaged Ben stepped inside.

"No more hiding," he bit out, grasping her soap-slickened shoulders. "And no more lying. Last night had nothing to do with moonlight, tropical air, or even just plain lust. Last night was between two people meant for each other in every way, and if you'd care to open your mind long enough to realize that you'd see the truth. Why not take the chance and see if we do have what it takes? What's so wrong with that?"

"What's wrong is you're just like my father!" she screamed back. "He spent every waking hour building up his business and didn't bother to take the time to enjoy life. He was so busy working on that next important deal, he died before he had a chance to savor his success. And I was racing down that same fast lane until something forced me to stop and realize what was happening to me. I was lucky and got out before it was too late. But you're doing the same thing my dad did. You'll keep on increasing the number of shops you own and work twenty-five hours a day at being the boss until you die at your desk too!" Her body was shaking so hard, her teeth chattered even though warm water was spilling all around her.

Ben understood her pain and where it was coming from. Because of how fast his business had grown and his talk of business trips and setting up new shops, Kelly saw him as a workaholic—whereas, in fact, he was far from it. Little did she know that he wasn't the kind of boss who had to have absolute control, that he believed in delegating responsibility to give himself time for himself.

Now all he had to do was show her that. He wrapped her in his arms.

"I guess there's only one thing to do, then,"

he said, sounding as bland as rice pudding while his body announced a dessert that was a great deal spicier.

She looked up, caramel eyes dark with suspicion. She didn't need it spelled out for her. The man's mind was obviously on one thing only. Still, being the businesswoman she was, she wanted to hear him spell it out, loud and clear. "Oh, really? And what is that?"

"I see I'm going to have to prove to you that, along with working hard when it's necessary, I've found ways to have more than enough time to enjoy life. I believe there's no reason why a person can't do both—and I'll just have to show you how it's done, won't I?"

FOUR

"Who does he think he is?" Kelly stood in front of her dresser mirror and pulled her brush through her hair with punishing speed. It didn't matter that the bristles caught in the tangles, bringing stinging tears to her eyes. The pain helped feed her agitation. She'd just thrown Ben out of her house and told him not to return, but the look in his eye told her he was going to whether she wanted him to or not. Not to mention his softly spoken promise that she wasn't going to get rid of him that easily. "Teach *me* a person can play and work effectively? I don't need him to teach me a thing! I can play with the best of them. And I certainly know all about working!"

He taught you there's more to lovemaking than

you ever thought possible, so there's a chance he does know more than you about effectively combining play and work, her traitorous brain chimed. *He showed you a side to yourself you never knew existed. Face it, Kelly, you liked it. Liked it a lot.*

"Stop telling me that!" she screamed at her hormone-laden mind. Resisting the urge to stamp her foot, she settled for throwing her brush across the room, where it bounced off a wall and fell to the floor. Sanity returned with a vengeance when she realized what she'd done. For a woman who neither lost her temper nor threw any kind of tantrum, because she secretly viewed them as spirit-draining, she was recently indulging her fury a few too many times for her peace of mind. And she knew exactly who to blame for that. She backed up until the end of her bed clipped her neatly against the backs of her knees, throwing her off balance. "Now I've really lost it," she moaned, dropping down onto the bed. "I'm yelling at myself. I came here for peace and quiet and now I'm acting like someone who's just escaped from the mental ward." After taking a deep breath, she stood up, pushed her hair away from her face, and strode into her workroom. Past experience had taught her that losing herself in a new creation would be the best way for her to regain her sanity.

"Why are you not here?" Lili demanded over the phone that evening the moment Kelly picked up the receiver.

It took a moment for the woman's question to register. "Your party is tonight."

"Yes, my party, which is going on right now, and you are very late," Lili scolded.

Kelly looked down at her paint-spattered T-shirt and shorts. There were even a few splotches of paint on her bare legs. "Lili, you can hate me all you want, but I'm not going to be able to make it. I've been painting all afternoon, and right now I'd like nothing more than a hot bath and an early evening in bed."

"No, I will not allow you to back out. I told you about this party weeks ago and you agreed to attend. I will give you a half hour, no more." She hung up before Kelly could phrase a protest.

"I guess I'm lucky she gave me *that* long," Kelly consoled herself.

Ben roamed the perimeter of the party, his

eyes slicing through the many people milling about, laughing and talking. There was no laughter in the brilliant emerald eyes as they sought the reason for his being there.

"She will be here soon. I gave her a half hour." Lili appeared at his elbow. She handed him a glass of champagne. "As usual, she lost herself in her work and forgot about the time."

An expression she couldn't quite catch flickered across his eyes. "Obviously, she doesn't know I'm here."

Lili cocked her head to one side. The petite woman was dressed in a white off-the-shoulder dress that displayed her deep tan to its best. Her dark hair was twisted back in a chignon to better show off her classic features. "There is something between you." She held up her hand. "I am not asking for answers, because I know I would not receive any, but it is not difficult to see you are interested in more than Kelly's designs." She tapped his forearm with a scarlet-tipped finger. "Drink your champagne and relax until she comes."

Ben felt as taut as a bowstring as he drank his champagne and tried to concentrate on a conversation among several men about Sydney's real estate market.

The tingling along the back of his neck was

the first indication. He turned slowly until he faced the patio door.

She was backlit by the lamps burning in the living room, creating a woman made of nothing more than light and shadow. Ben couldn't imagine how she had managed to make herself even more beautiful, but somehow she had accomplished just that.

Her black tissue faille jumpsuit molded lovingly over her slender curves, while the wide belt made her waist seem even smaller than it was. The long, sheer sleeves and satin collar bisecting the deep V-neckline only added to the illusion of sensuality. Her only items of jewelry were diamond eardrops that swung against her throat.

He snagged a second glass of champagne from a nearby tray and immediately headed for the doorway. The slight widening of Kelly's eyes when he appeared in her line of vision was her only sign of surprise at seeing him.

"My, my, you seem to know everyone on this island, don't you?" she asked dryly, stepping down as she accepted the proffered glass. Her fingertips tingled from the brief brush of his skin against hers.

"Lili took pity on me not knowing very many people on the island. She insisted that a relaxed atmosphere would be a good way to get to know my new neighbors," he explained, walking beside her.

She looked everywhere but at him as she walked across the patio, nodding and smiling as she went. "Lili is well known for sticking her nose in where it isn't wanted. I've warned her many times it's a good way to get it cut off, but she feels it's her duty in life to meddle where she can."

"*Cherie*, you're here!" Lili reached up and pressed her perfumed cheek against Kelly's.

A faint smile curved Kelly's lips. "Considering your telephone call, I didn't think I had a choice. You hate it when people miss your parties, and you always do such a lovely job of insuring they feel guilty for not attending. I can't afford the guilt."

"My dear, I would never allow you to feel guilty for anything and you know it." Lili stepped back and surveyed Kelly's outfit with frank satisfaction. "She is lovely, isn't she?" She looked up at Ben with a shrewd eye. "Too lovely to waste away on this island for the rest of her life."

"Yes." His reply was abstracted, since he was busy studying Kelly, his intentions explicit in his gaze. Being a Frenchwoman, Lili knew when it was time to leave. She smiled at Kelly, who was looking uncomfortable under Ben's bluntly speaking eyes, and quietly melted away.

"Stop it, Ben." Kelly glanced around to make sure no one else noticed his sensual absorption or overheard her words. She swallowed her drink in hopes of cooling the heat Ben's gaze generated, but the alcohol only intensified the liquid fire running through her veins.

"Stop what?"

"Stop looking at me as if you only want to get me into bed."

"That happened much too quickly, so now I'm standing back a little, to give you space." He spoke leisurely, looking as if the conversation was about nothing more innocuous than the weather. "Because I also want the chance to explore that mind of yours. I sense there's a great deal more to you than meets the eye, Kelly. I want to discover what caused you to hide away on this island, where you probably felt assured you wouldn't meet anyone. Aren't you lucky I came along when I did?" His smile was pure lethal male.

Her fingers tightened on the glass's stem. "Funny, I wouldn't have put it that way," she muttered, keeping a smile pasted on her rose-frosted lips. She'd never been more grateful for her years of dealing with the high and mighty of the finance world. No matter how chaotic her thoughts, she could look serene and unruffled.

Ben's eyes narrowed as a shield seemed to drop in front of Kelly's face. Her smile was bright and impersonal, her gaze as cool as if she were speaking to someone she'd just met that evening. He wanted to destroy that shield, force her to see what they could have together.

"Don't challenge me, Kelly, or I'll just have to pick up the gauntlet," he said softly.

She drew in a sharp breath. "I made no challenge."

"Oh, yes, you just made it. Right now, you're determined to treat me as a business associate, and nothing more. Although I can't think of any business associate of yours who would know about that tiny mole on your left breast, nor how you shiver in a man's arms and cry out when he enters you," he continued relentlessly, purposely ignoring her whitened features. "Of course, I have a feeling I've never traveled in the same business world as you did, so I could be wrong." With a brief nod, he walked away, not bothering to look back to see her reaction.

Kelly grabbed hold of her composure. There was no way she was going to allow anyone to see how strongly he affected her. Still, that didn't stop her from noticing how good he looked in tan slacks and a deep bronze short-sleeved shirt. She knew he was the kind of man who garnered interest no matter where he was. Such as the kind of interest a shapely redhead was now displaying by leaning much too close to Ben as she spoke.

"Your jealousy is showing, *cherie*," Lili scolded, placing a hand on her arm. "You know how Desiree is when there's a new man around. She always feels she must show her charms."

"Oh yes, she has to see how much testosterone she can milk from a man. She's the ultimate black widow," Kelly said dryly. "Did we ever figure out how many notches she has on her bedpost?"

"Only a computer could keep track. Now come with me and have some food." In Lili's mind, food healed any hurt known to man, or woman.

For the rest of the evening, no matter where Kelly was, who she spoke to, Ben wasn't all that far behind. He neither joined in on any of her conversations nor approached her again, but her sensitive nerve endings were constantly aware of his presence. That, along with memories of the night they'd spent together, was more than enough to unsettle her. The hot feel of his skin against hers, his mouth tracing erotic patterns everywhere, the explicit words he'd whispered in her ear just before he'd turned those words into deeds. These were memories she didn't want to recall.

She suddenly couldn't breathe, couldn't draw air into her lungs. She smiled, murmured a few words about the smoke bothering her eyes, and quickly moved toward the edge of the patio that led to the beach. She slipped off her black pumps, dropped them to one side, and walked on the sand toward the water's edge, seeking something she wasn't even sure she'd recognize if she found it. She tipped her face back, feeling the ocean breeze cool her skin and senses.

"Amazing. A woman who can look exciting in the moonlight whether she's clothed or not."

She looked to her right. "Why are you doing this?" Her whispered words floated on the breeze.

"Because I believe in finishing something already begun."

The coil of hair on her head seemed suddenly heavy. She reached up with one hand and pulled out the pins, causing waves of hair to cascade down her back. Her diamond earrings winked brightly in the moonlight.

"Ben, you are a very nice man, you have a business that's growing all the time, and you are an incredible lover, but my life is very carefully mapped out, and a man doesn't enter into it," she said bluntly. "If you don't like it, that's your problem, not mine. If you don't care to do any more business with me, fine. Just please understand that I don't want a lover in my life."

"Is there anything wrong with having a friend in it?"

He'd again thrown her off balance. "A friend?"

His smile was slightly crooked and endearing. In her eyes, this was much more a danger than any passionate words could be. "You know, a buddy. Someone to talk to when the problems of the world get to be too much, go swimming with, explore the island on days off—all those good things."

Amusement put sparkles in her eyes.

"Somehow I can't visualize you as a woman's buddy. You just don't fit the picture."

"Why not find out what I can be?" he softly urged, moving forward two steps. "Come on, Kelly. Give it a try. What harm can it do?"

It could be the ruin of all my inner peace, she thought to herself, unable to stop staring at him. She felt herself weaken. "No sex." She made her voice cool and firm, as if wrapping up a business deal.

That crooked grin reappeared as he held out his hand to shake hers. "No sex," he readily agreed. He took her arm and escorted her back to the party. "Of course, if you seduce *me*, all bets are off."

She shook her head in wonderment. "Now why am I not surprised that you managed to get in the last word?"

"Because I believe in playing to win."

"This isn't a game."

"No, it's much more important than that."

As she walked with him, she wondered just what she was allowing herself to get into. And if she would still have her sanity when it was all over.

"I need your help."

Kelly rubbed eyes that felt gritty from staying up until early-morning hours and drinking too much champagne. She'd thought she could dull her senses from Ben's visual lovemaking at Lili's party. All she'd managed to do was end up with a headache and bloodshot eyes. She did not expect to wake up to a ringing phone and Ben's mesmerizing voice at the other end of it, caressing her sleep-fogged senses.

"What time is it?" she mumbled, struggling to find her clock and finally giving up.

"A little after nine. Are you still in bed?"

"Of course I'm still in bed. Where else would a civilized being be at this hour when she stayed at a party until two because her hostess refused to let her go home?" She patted her hand against her open mouth. "Try me again in two hours, when I feel more human." A deep groan echoed in her ear. "What's wrong? Are you feeling sick?"

"Far from it. I'm aroused at the memory of you in that bed with the sheets in disarray around your lovely body," he said roughly.

Kelly was struck dumb by his blunt words. She shifted in the bed, suddenly aware of the slide of the sheets across her bare skin and the cool caress of the fabric. "If this is an obscene phone call, Wyatt, you've called the wrong party," she finally told him.

"What I'm thinking of is far from obscene. No, I called because I need your help for my new store," he replied. "Wear something casual and I'll pick you up in fifteen minutes."

"Fifteen minutes?" The moment she sputtered the words she knew it wouldn't do any good. He'd already hung up without giving her a chance to refuse. "If he thinks I'm going anywhere with him, he has another think coming. What makes him think I can just take off on a whim? I have my day planned."

By Kelly's watch, Ben arrived fourteen minutes, thirty-seven seconds later. She took him at his word and chose a pair of khaki walking shorts and a burnt orange sleeveless crop top that revealed a band of lightly tanned flesh, and pulled her hair up in a ponytail tied with a scarf the same color as her top. She'd been determined to be ready when he arrived, and she made it with twenty seconds to spare.

"Considering the number of stores you've already opened, I would think you'd have it all down to a science by now," she greeted him.

"Since I make each one unique, I always like to get a second opinion." He held out both hands. One contained a plastic cup filled with rich, steaming coffee, the other a rich yellow and orange streaked rose.

Kelly stared at both, unsure which to reach for first. She gave in and took the rose. "This isn't from anywhere on the island," she said huskily, smiling when she smelled the haunting fragrance it gave off.

He was pleased she admired his offering. "It pays to have connections. The coffee is a peace offering for waking you up before you were ready to face the world, and the rose is because I felt it was almost as lovely as you are." His eyes skimmed over her outfit with alarming thoroughness. "It appears my choice of color was appropriate."

Kelly carried the rose inside to find her crystal bud vase.

"You certainly know how to get a lady's attention," she told him over her shoulder. "Is this little touch something you do for all your women, or do you use a different technique for each one? It must be impossible for you to keep track of what you've done for whom. Do you keep it all in a little book or on computer?" She hadn't bothered inviting him inside. She knew he would come in, either way. Sure enough, he was right on her heels as she entered the kitchen and rummaged through her cabinets until she found her vase.

He looked more than a little disgruntled as he leaned against the counter watching her fill the vase with water and carefully place the rose inside. "I don't believe in collecting women, nor do I have anything close to a black book," he told her in clipped tones. "And, no, this is not a habit with me, usually because my social life is a bit limited. You seem to enjoy trying to keep me at arm's length with these little quips of yours. By now, you should know they won't work. I have a pretty thick hide."

She plucked the coffee cup out of his hand and sipped the hot brew. She closed her eyes, relishing the swift rush of caffeine in her veins. She hoped it would help keep her on her toes where Ben was concerned. "I don't need quips to keep you at arm's length, just the right amount of indifference," she murmured. "I figure the time will come when you'll realize the interest isn't returned and you'll head off for greener pastures."

Ben stole the cup out of her hand and placed it on the counter, then pulled her into his arms. "You delight in baiting me, Kelly, and saying you're indifferent. I see it different-ly." His body tightened with arousal as he realized her silky cotton top was molding not a bra cup, but bare skin. He kept his hands on her waist—with great effort, since he wanted nothing more than to place them under her clothing and reexplore that lovely skin. "Amazing how an indifferent woman could respond so quickly, isn't it?" His eyes, when he raised them to hers, gleamed a brilliant green.

"It's nothing more than an involuntary response." She silently damned the fact that her voice had turned huskier than usual. Where was her hard-boiled-businesswoman facade when she needed it?

Ben looked down at Kelly's breasts as they rose and fell in an agitated manner. "Is that why you're also flushed and trying very hard not to touch me? Why your skin appears warm and your scent is heightened? Involuntary responses are amazing, aren't they?"

If he'd meant to get her temper up, he accomplished just that. She placed her open palms against his chest and pushed, hard. "I think this would be a perfect time for us to leave."

"Afraid if we stay I'll talk you into bed?"

She moved past him with incredible speed. "I've already figured out you'd try to do a great deal more than talk," she said dryly. "All right,

Man from Down Under, let's check into those so-called problems you're having with your shop." She marched toward the front door, confident he would follow.

Kelly walked outside, not surprised to discover that Ben had commandeered one of the small Jeeps that were kept for the hotel staff's use on the resort's grounds. She sensed he'd had no trouble sweet-talking a bemused hotel employee—female, of course—into allowing him the use of one of the hotel's vehicles. After all, he seemed to have had no trouble talking her into going with him now!

"What trouble, exactly, are you having?" she began without preamble once they were speeding along the bumpy road. She slipped her oversize sunglasses on and jammed an orange baseball cap on her head.

Ben took his eyes off the road for a brief second. He'd never known a woman who could look so vibrant or act with such love for life as Kelly did. He wondered again what had brought her to this island. "As I explained earlier, each shop is different, decorated to go with the theme of the island it's on. Our Waikiki shop is very trendy, the one on Kona more laid-back, very 'island traditional' if there is such a phrase, and the one in Tahiti is even more traditional. I want to explore the island, see its little-known spots for inspiration, and I felt you would be the perfect guide."

She settled back in the seat. "That's a job for a decorator. Don't you have one on retainer?"

"I used to look for someone in the area, until I found out most of them didn't believe the client could be right sometimes. And trying to find someone on a permanent basis isn't as easy as I'd like." He grimaced. "My most recent decorator left after I told her these shops should embody a tropical island flavor, not New York's. She was talking hot pink and black with strobe lights and heavy metal music."

"That sounds more appropriate for downtown Hollywood!" she burst out, horrified at the idea. "I hope you sent her back to New York where she belonged."

He rubbed the side of his nose with his fingertip as he murmured, "Actually, she'd grown up in a remote part of New Zealand."

She laughed at his admission. "Then she must have watched too many movies from the disco era to think up strobe lights and hot pink walls."

"I guess I could keep her in mind if we ever open a store in Hollywood."

"That would be a major error."

"Why?"

She twisted in the seat and rested her back against the door. "First off, there's too many clothing shops vying for business there. Second, you carry specialty items meant for a slower way of life. Oh, I'm certain your customers still wear their purchases once they're back home, but there they're something special, unique. Which means that when their friends travel out this way, they'll stop in to see what unique items you have for them. Keep yourself specialized and you can continue to command the higher prices; shoot for a broader market and you lose the exclusivity that brings in your higher-income-bracket customers. There's nothing these ladies like more than paying a high price for something they know their friends don't have in their closets."

"You have a good grasp of the retail business. Is that what you did before you moved here?" he probed delicately—but not delicately enough to escape Kelly's notice.

She bestowed on him the kind of smile a mother gives a precocious son. "Next time you go fishing, try a better bait."

His sweeping glance covered her from head to toe, lingering just a fraction longer than elsewhere on her bare legs. He idly wondered if her toes still sported that sexy peach nail polish he remembered from that night. Come to think of it, he remembered a lot from that night: the way she felt in his arms, the way she cried out when she shattered in a climax that tore them both apart, the way she looked at him as if there was no one else in the world for her. He silently cursed her for trying to ignore what they'd once shared—and could undoubtedly share again, if she would just lower that damn stubborn wall she'd erected against him. Still, he considered her coming with him today a step in the right direction.

"What new creations are you going to design for this shop?" he asked, deciding it might be a good time to divert the conversation to business. He'd concentrate on personal matters later, when they were in a better-suited atmosphere.

"I'd like to work with silk more, even if it is a bit risky," she replied, switching topics as easily as he had. "I thought of working on some sarongs, skirts, and tops. Maybe dresses with designs painted on the skirt only or along the hemline. I've found some beautiful citrus colors that always look cool and comfortable. I sometimes employ some talented local seamstresses when I want to work on a design I can't find."

"I've noticed how much your work has advanced from your first designs. You seem to have grown more daring by using different techniques. One of my secretaries has taken some fabric-painting classes, and she said you don't seem to follow any rules."

"There aren't any rules," she explained. "I just follow my instinct for whatever seems right with a particular piece of clothing. It's the same method a wood-carver or sculptor might use." She'd discovered that by remaining propped against the door, she could study Ben's profile from behind the safety of her sunglasses without his noticing. A bit craggy, she silently decided. She doubted he'd ever visited the dentist to have caps put on his teeth or used a tanning salon to keep his skin a rich color or had a personal trainer come to see him three times a week to keep his body in shape. It was evident he was the kind of man who wouldn't be bothered with the fakery other men used to make themselves look better to the opposite sex. How many men had she dealt with in the past who had manicures more often than she did?

All of this worried her. For too long she'd been happy without a man in her life—until that night she'd made love with Ben. And no matter how much she argued with herself, she knew it had been making love, and not just a night of hot sex.

What was it about Ben that fascinated her so much? She feared it was her heart more than her logical brain that carried the answer.

FIVE

Kelly crossed the lush square of grass until she stood at the edge of a blue pool of water where she could easily study the waterfall as it dropped its silvery cascade. Keeping her hands folded behind her back, she turned around. This was the stance of Kelly Andrews, savvy businesswoman, not Kelly, the woman of the islands who believed in taking life one day at a time.

"I have to say, I'm very impressed with your decorator's skills, Mr. Wyatt," she drawled, holding out one hand to gesture to the pool. "And you claim she wasn't talented. Why, she turned your shop into a tropical oasis, complete with pool. Tell me, was this done with holographic images or just plain old-fashioned painted backdrops?"

Ben plucked a picnic basket out of the back of the Jeep and carried it to the grass that lined the pool. "Actually, it's all done with mirrors. I discovered this spot when I drove around the island yesterday," he explained, setting the basket down and opening it. "While I wouldn't mind having a boutique with this atmosphere, I don't think we'd have any luck getting the customers to leave."

Her smile began by curving her lips upward before traveling higher to her eyes. "Not all of them. Just those who prefer a false facade to the real thing."

"Like people who live on the beach but have a swimming pool in their backyard. Hey, you better come over and get your share before I eat it all," he teased.

Kelly walked over and knelt down so she could better inspect the basket's contents. She oohed and aahed as she inspected containers holding fresh fruit salad, tart, bite-size pieces of pineapple chicken kept warm in an insulated container, sesame rolls, and other palate-tempting and attractively packaged treats.

"This all looks too good to eat," she sighed,

admiring the feast Ben had laid before her. "But I'll force myself."

"I thought since I'd probably robbed you of your breakfast I should make it up to you with a special lunch." Ben opened the bottle of white wine he'd pulled out of the basket and filled two glasses, handing one to her. "This might not be as good as the Mexican lunch you prepared for me, but it's filling."

"Not as good? Are you kidding?" She stole a slice of mango and nibbled on it. "Most of the time, if I even remember lunch, I settle for some fruit or a few glasses of juice in hopes it will hold me until dinnertime."

Ben frowned. No wonder she was so thin! "That's not very healthy. I may not be the best with my eating habits, but I do try to eat three decent meals. Otherwise, I'm impossible to work with. At least, that's what my secretary says."

Her soft laughter washed over him like a summer rain. "Believe me, it's much more healthy than what I used to consume. Once upon a time I was known to live on nothing but coffee and cigarettes for days. I ignored the burning stomach and insomnia, just as I ignored what I was doing to my body back then. Now I gorge on healthier food, even if

I do occasionally indulge in midnight feasts when I whip up brownies or a pan of fudge." She filled two plates with a little of everything and handed one to Ben. "I also make a mean fudge torte when my chocolate cravings get out of hand. Trouble is, I usually eat the whole thing in one sitting. Unless I can get my hands on Goo Goo Clusters. Then it's no holds barred and no one gets between me and those wonderful goodies." Her eyes took on a hazy gleam.

"Goo Goo what?"

"Goo Goo Clusters. Caramel, marshmallow, and peanuts, all covered in milk chocolate," she explained. "I discovered them a few years ago when I was on a business trip to the midwest. California didn't have them in most stores, but I did some searching and sometimes got lucky. They're my real weakness."

Ben picked up a piece of chicken from his plate and held it out to Kelly. She leaned forward, taking it carefully between her lips. "And here I thought *I* was your weakness," he murmured, selecting a slice of papaya to offer her next.

This time, she pretended to ignore his intent and dug into her own plate of food as she settled herself more comfortably by sitting cross-legged across from him. "You lied to me, didn't you? You had no plans to talk about your shop." She stated it as a fact.

"Correct," he stated without any sign of guilt. "I wanted to have you all to myself, with no mention of business, and this seemed the best place for us to talk without any interruptions."

Try as she might, Kelly couldn't conjure up any anger at this blatant admission. "I'd heard Australian men were brash and incorrigible. You've certainly lived up to your reputation," she said, then added softly, "Thank you."

This confused him. "For what?"

"For being honest just now. I'm sure you could have come up with a plausible answer, but you didn't. You told me the truth, all the while knowing you were taking a chance. I might have become so angry with you I'd demand you take me home this minute. Of course, I'd have insisted we wait until I finished eating." She finished her fruit and turned her attention back to the chicken. "Good thing you brought along the food. I can't be angry with a man who feeds me."

He felt unsure about what was happening. Just when he thought he could keep her off balance, here she was turning the tables on him! "You can't?"

"Of course not." She favored him with another one of those smiles that always seemed to go to his head like a fine wine. "Because there is no way I would stand up and walk away from all of this. Especially since I haven't had dessert yet, which appears to be the resort chef's special coconut cream cake, with a rich filling that literally melts in one's mouth. But you do deserve punishment, so I guess you'll have to give up your share of it." She kept her hand on the container holding the cake.

Ben wasn't sure whether to laugh or just gape at her in astonishment. "I'll accept any punishment but giving up the cake," he said finally. "I've tasted it before, and nothing will force me to give up my share."

She beamed, very sure of herself. "We'll see."

"Is this how you dealt with people in your past life? You must have been one hell of a negotiator in the boardroom."

Kelly stilled. She looked down at her plate, the bill of her cap effectively hiding her features. "What makes you think I dealt in big business? I could have been a clerk, a typist, or a receptionist for a storefront office. Perhaps a secretary."

He shook his head. "Executive administrative assistant, maybe, but you're not the type to take orders when you can give them. You're too poised, too sure of your words. It's the way you carry yourself and the way you've negotiated your past contracts with us. Only a woman very familiar with the ins and outs of contract terminology could strike the deals you have. You never had to think about what to say. You knew what you wanted and you made sure to achieve that goal, or as close to it as possible."

She looked wary. She didn't know why, since she really had nothing to hide. She just preferred to forget that part of her life and to continue on with her new one. "Why is my past work experience so important to you? I can assure you it has nothing to do with what's going on now. Boardrooms and fabric painting don't mix, trust me."

He leaned forward and brushed a stray curl away from her face, securing it behind her ear. "Why is it so wrong to talk about your past? Is it a crime that I want to know everything about you, Kelly? And don't close yourself up," he ordered gently, watching her shut her thoughts off from him. Strange, he thought to himself, how easily he could read her now. How he always seemed to sense what was going on behind those unusual-color eyes. So much was happening between them, he had trouble understanding it all. "I'm more than willing to tell you everything you want to know about me." He held his arms open to show he felt he had nothing to hide.

She considered his offer. "All right, tell me about the first girl you kissed."

"Brianne Miller. She was six, I was an adult seven who talked her into playing doctor. She didn't like my kisses and pushed me in a mud puddle. I never got over her," he sadly finished.

Kelly bit her lower lip to keep from laughing. "Your first pet."

"Mildred. She was a very sweet iguana. . . . She was!" he insisted when he saw her wrinkle her nose in distaste.

"The first woman you fell in love with." She leaned back on her elbows, confident that was a subject no man would talk about with another woman.

His eyes darkened to pure jade as his thoughts reverted to the past. "Lisa Burrows. Long brown hair, beautiful blue eyes, a voice that sounded so musical. She seemed to gather up sunlight to give out on gloomy days." Kelly straightened up. Ben's declaration of his one true love wasn't something she'd expected to hear—nor, to be honest, something she'd wanted to. "She made the world sound like such a magical place that I used to wish I could see her for more than an hour a day." His voice drifted off. "She taught geography."

"A teacher?" Her voice squeaked.

"You asked about the first woman I fell in love with. I may have been only fourteen at the time, but I knew I was in love with her," he declared with a solemn expression. "It was the only class I consistently received high marks in, because I didn't want to disappoint her. The day she announced her engagement was the saddest of my life, but I soon picked myself up and went on to love again."

The latter words were softly spoken and laden with a meaning that brought deep color to Kelly's cheeks. Ben inwardly cheered. The lady knew only too well what he was talking about, and she hadn't been able to hide behind her cool, calm facade quickly enough. He picked up her hand and idly fiddled with her fingers. Her skin was smooth to the touch, the fingers long, the nails manicured and sporting a sheer cinnamon polish. When he turned her hand over, he found a tiny smudge of bright pink in the crease of one of her fingers.

"Sometimes fabric paint isn't too easy to wash off," she explained, her voice husky.

Ben kept her hand prisoner as he tipped his head back to be able to look more easily at her. "I never met a woman who tries as hard as you do to keep your emotions under wraps," he commented.

"Don't try to figure me out, Ben," she murmured, curling her fingers around his palm. "It will only strain a brain that I'm sure is already overtaxed, with all you're doing."

He tightened his hold on her hand and slowly pulled her downward until her face hovered just above his. "Your heart rate just sped up, your skin is growing warmer, and your nipples—which I recall as a lovely shade of deep peach—are tightening at the thought of our lying in the grass and making love."

For a moment, she lost all conscious thought as she tried to keep her breathing as steady as possible, even though it meant inhaling the musky fragrance of man coupled with the lime scent of the soap he must have used that morning.

"For a businessman, you have an incredible imagination," she finally said, forcing the words out.

He smiled. "Do I? Think about it, Kelly: the two of us lying over there in grass thick enough to be a luxury mattress. My slipping off your clothes. You taking off mine. Our having the chance to see what we missed seeing that night. While moonlight is all right for making love, sunlight is much better. And it's the perfect day for it."

A heavy liquid thrummed its way through her veins as his words took root in her mind and she began to visualize all he was talking about. Their taking off each other's clothes, her touching him the way she had that night, his touching her, arousing her. . . . until all she could think of was his body merged with hers.

"Ben," was all she could manage to say this time. "I told you before that it's not a good idea."

"What, our making love? Or just talking about it?" he countered. "Tell me, Kelly, what's so wrong with our giving each other pleasure?"

Her eyes dropped until they encountered the masculine bulge, which seemed to pulse as her fingers hesitantly touched the coarse fabric of his clothing, then slid slowly toward the place that mesmerized her so.

"Kelly, don't torture me," he said hoarsely, grasping her chin in a harsh grip and forcing her face upward.

"I won't deny I'm still very confused about what's happening between us, because I'm also trying to understand something I've never experienced before," she murmured, smiling wanly at the gleam of hope that sprang to his eyes. "I'm being honest, Ben, because I don't believe in running away from the truth." She inwardly flinched at her blatant lie. She had run away from the truth once because a part of her hadn't wanted to face it. If only she had known she had no reason to flee back then, she thought now, even as she acknowledged that it was the best thing she'd ever done for herself.

Ben twisted his body, following Kelly down onto the grass. "When I'm around you, I discover it's not easy to go slow," he told her, carefully pulling off her cap and loosening her ponytail from its clip. He finger-combed the thick strands until they lay in delicious disarray on the grass.

"It sounds like you need therapy."

He concentrated on the tawny strands of hair spilling between his fingers. "I don't think I want to be cured."

"Ben, I told you before: I'm not into fast-and-furious affairs," she warned. "I'm also not pushing for any kind of commitment, because it's too soon to even think of such a thing, if ever it comes to that. But I won't allow you to push me. I have a lot of things to work out within myself, and involvement with a man who runs a demanding business such as you have can't be part of my life."

His features tightened at her cool tone. "For a woman who appears to be as intuitive as you are, you seem to have more than a few blind spots where people are concerned. You like to pigeonhole people, Kelly, although you seem to forget that some people just aren't going to fit into the rigid compartments you want them to. Think about it: If I were the driven businessman you claim I am, we wouldn't be having lunch here, we would be having it in the hotel dining room—if I'd even bothered taking the time out to call and ask you to meet me." He levered himself up off her and sat back. "There's something happening between us. Why do you work so hard to deny it?"

His demand made her see red. She snatched up her baseball cap and jammed it on her head, not caring that her hair flew wildly around her face. She jumped to her feet and began pacing back and forth. "Why do you have to work so hard to insist on the impossible?"

"Because I don't want to lose you."

"You can't lose something you've never had!"

"But I have had you."

His quietly spoken statement stopped her cold. She took several deep breaths in hopes of slowing her anger.

"That's not fair."

He cocked an eyebrow. "At least you don't try to insist it never happened or blame it on the moonlight or your hormones. But then, you did try to blame it on hormones, didn't you?"

Kelly jammed her fingers through her hair, not even noticing that her movements dislodged her cap. "There's so many things you don't know," she sighed.

"Then tell me. Make me understand why you keep pushing me away." His pleading tone touched something inside her. "Kelly, I can't remember the last time I felt this way about a woman, if ever. And I know you feel the same way. I can see it in your eyes, in the way you look at me. I'm not a vain man, just a very confused one. I'm sure I'm not the first man to feel like this where you're concerned," he said wryly, beginning to pack up the containers and put them back in the basket.

Kelly hated to feel like a fool, which was exactly what she felt like. She turned around to face the pool, because she wasn't sure she could say what she wanted to if she were still facing him.

"There's a very good reason for the way I feel, Ben. And not just because of my father. I worked in a very high-powered, fast-paced area of high finance. I was a senior partner in a Los Angeles-based financial consulting firm that boasted clients from around the world. I could strike a deal for millions of dollars and not blink an eye. I knew many of the movers and shakers of the world's financial community on a first-name basis and could dial their private line by memory. In fact, my mind was known as a computer because of the facts and figures it stored," she said in a low voice.

"I was one of the few women in what was basically a man's business, and I loved it. I loved the pressure and the wheeling and dealing so much, it almost killed me. By all rights, I should be dead now." She deliberately ignored the stunned expression that crossed Ben's face. "The reason I ended up here was because my doctor told me I didn't have long to live, when

all I'd wanted him to do was give me something for the headaches, the constant heart-
burn, and the insomnia I suffered all the time.
When he told me I had about eighteen months
to live, I felt as if a wall had crashed down on
me. All I knew was that I didn't want to die
at my desk, with everyone saying they knew it
couldn't have happened any other way because
the business was as much in my blood as it had
been in my father's. I felt I had to do something with my life before it was too late." Kelly
felt Ben's shock roll over her like a crashing
wave. Just as she felt him stand up, walk over
to her, and rest his hands on her shoulders.

"What did the doctor say you have?" It was
as if the words had been forced from him, as if
he wanted to deny what he'd just heard. Could
the woman he'd just found and fallen in love
with be taken away from him that quickly?
"There's always hope, Kelly. Doctors all over
the world are coming up with options. Did you
ever seek any of them out? All right, I may not
know you long, but I already know you're not
one to just close yourself off until it's all over.
You're a fighter, not one to just sit back and
take what the world gives out."

She shook her head and laughed, but the
sound held no humor. "I was told there was no

hope, and I don't believe in hanging on to false promises, which was why I took off for parts unknown. Being poked and prodded by doctors for months on end wasn't my idea of fun. It turned out I didn't have to worry. I guess you'd call it an error in my favor, although it meant someone else wasn't as lucky. It turned out the test results for another woman with a similar name were somehow mixed up with mine at the lab. I was given her diagnosis."

She turned to face him. "While all this was going on—and before I found out I wasn't dying—I was in the midst of finalizing a nasty divorce. I was tired and stressed out all the time, and I knew I had to get away before the men in the white coats came to get me. So I sold my partnership in the agency and left everything in the hands of my attorney, then took off."

She touched his arm, willing him to understand why she had handled things the way she had. "One thing I was certain of was that I didn't want to die in my office and that I didn't want to see pity in anyone's eyes if they found out about my illness. I was more comfortable with strangers who knew nothing about me, and I soon discovered there was more to myself than I ever thought. After a few months bumming around the South Pacific, I ended up here. It didn't take me long to realize this was where I was meant to be. It's only been recently that I've learned about the error in the medical records, so I'm still dealing with that and grieving for the woman who didn't have the chance I did to prepare herself." She silently pleaded with him. "Now do you understand why I'm the way I am? I was given my life a second time, and I don't intend to blow it."

He shook his head, unable to take in all the information she had just thrown at him. "I always was a pushy bastard," he ruefully admitted. "I've told you I'm more than willing to be friends, and before you know it I'm trying to entice you into bed. No wonder you want to keep your distance from me. Just consider it part of my heritage. We Aussie men tend to go after what we want, without thinking of the consequences. All right, we'll do it your way. When I go overboard, you just remind me. And if you don't . . ." His ear-to-ear grin told her that if she didn't, it would be all her fault!

"You are incorrigible," she said without heat. "Why do I put up with this? Why am I allowing myself to go nuts just listening to you?" Her question was rhetorical.

"Because I'm lovable and you can't resist me?" he prompted with an uplifted brow.

She braced her hand on her hip and cocked her head to one side as she studied him. She had to admit, no man had ever gotten to her the way he had. "Maybe." She was only going to admit so much. "Honestly, Mr. Wyatt, with that kind of ego you should have a head the size of Texas!"

"Ah, ah, ah, Australia," he corrected. "Texas has nothing on the size of Australia."

"How could I forget." Her lips couldn't stop curving upward. "How do you do it, Ben? How do you sway me from wanting to murder you to wanting to . . ." Her voice trailed off.

"Make love to me? Or maybe just a few hot and heavy kisses?" He took a chance and rested his hands on her hips. She didn't move away, but he wasn't about to take any chances on going further. As far as he was concerned, he had all the time in the world.

Kelly couldn't help it. She looped her arms around his neck, which carried her forward until her breasts brushed lightly against his chest. "You're doing it again."

"Being overbearing?"

"And pushy and egocentric and . . ." She looked heavenward for verbal assistance.

"And the best thing that could come into a woman's life. Aren't you glad to be that lucky woman?" He slowly moved his hands up until they cupped the sides of her waist.

She tapped her forefinger against his chest. "If I had any sense I would turn around and run as far from you as possible."

A faint flicker appeared in her eyes. Ben wasn't sure if she was starting to think those nasty rational thoughts again, but he wasn't about to allow that to happen.

"Don't run," he murmured, dipping his head and running his tongue across her lower lip. He could taste the wine she'd drunk, smell the light perfume that was headier than any alcohol he could drink. "Stay."

Her lips parted under his touch. "And play?" she breathed.

His mouth settled more firmly on hers. "And play." The words ticked between them like a time bomb. "With me. I'm a wonderful playmate."

Her fingertips dug into his nape as she allowed herself to be swept under the crashing wave of his kiss. Ben slid his hands under the silky top to caress even silkier skin, which warmed immediately under fingers that were soon moving around to cup a bare breast.

"The moment I realized you weren't wearing a bra, I wanted to drive back to your house and keep you to myself," he told her in a ragged voice. "But I know that's the kind of man you don't want. I'll be honest: I'm not usually attracted to independent women. But I'm quickly discovering I've missed out on something powerful. I don't intend to let you slip through my fingers now."

Her eyes bored into his, searching for the glib lies she was so used to hearing from men. "Then we're even, because I'm not used to men who speak so honestly."

"Do you agree we should investigate this more thoroughly?" His lips gently rubbed against hers.

Her smile warmed his mouth. "I suppose it would be the thing to do, wouldn't it?"

"By all means."

SIX

"Did you have final approval for this space or was it handled by one of your staff?" Kelly stood in the middle of the empty shop, turning slowly to view the area from all sides. Nothing in her expression indicated her inner thoughts as her brain tucked away all that she saw.

"Actually, it was handled by one of my department heads who finds new shop spaces for us when we decide it's time to expand again," Ben replied from his spot in one corner, where he leaned against the wall with his arms crossed in front of his chest.

"What are you paying for it, and is it by square footage or a flat fee?" She frowned when she heard the amount. "And you've signed the paperwork?"

He shook his head. "I'm doing that tomorrow afternoon. We had to hold off because the hotel owner wanted to be present. Although everyone in this part of the world knows my word is as good as my signature."

Her mind continued to click away like the computer it was. She circled the shop space. "Do you have a copy of the contract with you?"

Ben ducked his head to hide his grin. "It's in my suite."

She nodded, turning toward the open door. "Good, I want to see how much of a mess your manager got you into."

Ben had no choice but to follow her long stride through the lobby. When he'd suggested they look at his shop space, he'd had no idea she'd pounce on the idea and want to leave at that very moment. The picnic basket had been duly packed up and they'd headed for the hotel without further ado.

"Kelly, I have an excellent legal department that looks over all the contracts very closely," he reminded her as they entered the elevator and he inserted his key card for one of the two penthouse floors.

"Lawyers tend to see only what they want to see or what you want them to see, not necessarily what's good for you," she informed him. "Believe me, I know, because my best friend is an attorney, and she once told me just that. She said the joke about sharks not attacking lawyers because of professional courtesy is very true."

The elevator door slid silently open to reveal a marble-floored foyer that led directly into the sitting room. Kelly didn't raise an eyebrow at the opulence of the suite. She crossed the foyer to an inlaid dining room table.

"Have many formal dinners here?" She crossed the room, unerringly finding the bar, where she pulled out two bottles of soda and poured them into two squat lead-crystal glasses. She sat at the head of the table, setting the glasses down.

"Not if I can help it." Ben disappeared into one of the bedrooms and returned carrying a leather briefcase. He pulled out a thick sheaf of papers and placed them in front of her. "You'll see it's all very cut-and-dried and to my advantage."

Kelly reached into her purse and pulled out a pair of reading glasses before surveying the paperwork. "Do you have a pad of paper around?" She was immediately immersed in the intricate wording and didn't notice when a legal pad and pen appeared by her elbow.

Ben watched as she carefully read the fine print of each page, only stopping occasionally to jot down a few words. He knew he was now seeing the businesswoman who must have intimidated more than a few men. He was grateful he wasn't easily intimidated, and wondered why he hadn't heard her name before. He could only figure that he'd been too involved with his shops to think about the world of finance. He settled back and enjoyed himself by studying her facial expressions, which were few, proving she knew what to display and what not to. How many more sides to Kelly was he going to discover? So far, he'd found much more than he'd ever expected to find in one woman.

It took Kelly more than two hours to study the contract. When she finished, she pulled off her glasses and placed them on the table. With her hands folded in front of her and her face set in a serious expression, she looked all business.

"Let's talk about all those nasty little clauses your legal department seems to have overlooked," she began without preamble, then spoke at length about some of the fees listed in the contract that should be paid by the hotel, not Ben. She jabbed her pen into the pad, pointing out sections she didn't agree with and questioning him at length.

"I had no idea how little I knew about this part of the business," he murmured, alternately impressed with the sharp precision of her comments and embarrassed at how few of her questions he could reasonably answer. "I had no idea how many of the day-to-day tasks I was allowing my staff to perform without my keeping up with them." He shook his head. "I guess since the business has expanded so much, most of my attention is required at a corporate level, making it hard to keep up with what everyone else is doing."

Kelly studied some of the notes she'd made. "Does your staff hand in weekly updates to you?"

Ben shifted in his chair. "They do it monthly."

She easily guessed the reason behind his unease. "Do you read them?"

"About once a year. I trust my staff implicitly. If I didn't I wouldn't feel comfortable enough to leave the office for any length of time," he argued.

"Considering how quickly your business

has grown, you have to trust the people who work directly under you, but you also need to know what they're doing, before it's too late." She ignored his glower. "I'm not attacking you, Ben. I'm just pointing out some of the mistakes I've made in the past and things I learned from my dad. One piece of advice he passed on to me was that weekly, if not daily, reports from each department head are necessary to keep the boss updated as to what's going on. Even if they only fill out a preprinted form, it's something. If you'd seen them first, I don't think you would have allowed some of these clauses to get past you."

She tapped the top sheet of paper with her finger. "I'll be honest with you, Ben. They're really not in your favor. While they look good from a legal standpoint, they're really not all that good from a business standpoint. It will cut into your profits drastically, because you're making payments where you shouldn't have to."

Ben shook his head. "How do you do it?"

She shrugged. "Practice."

"No, that's not what I mean. How do you make me feel like an idiot one moment, then stroke my ego the next?"

She smiled. "Unfortunately, equal opportunity isn't all that common in big business, so a woman needs to learn from the beginning how to do that. And, as I said before, I had my dad for a teacher, from the moment he discovered I had an affinity for finance. He was a better advisor regarding the classes I needed than the one I had in college. Dad had me taking some heavy-duty business law courses along with all the finance and accounting classes. My firm dealt heavily in the real estate market, so these kinds of contracts are pretty much run-of-the-mill for me, and I picked up more expertise along the way."

She was starting to feel a bit disconcerted that her suggestions might have backfired. When she'd offered to look at his contract, she hadn't thought that he might not appreciate her picking out the weak spots. Still, she said firmly, "I won't apologize for stating the truth."

"Why should you apologize?" he demanded. "From what you've just told me, I'm going to save money, right?"

She nodded, looking wary. "Right."

"And this is basically in my favor, right?"

She hoped she didn't look confused by his

questions. Didn't this man like good news? "Naturally."

Ben jumped up and snatched her out of her chair, swinging her in a circle.

"Ben, put me down. I'm getting dizzy!" she laughingly announced, gripping his shoulders to keep herself as secure as possible.

He set her back down on her feet, but kept his hands on her waist. "Kelly, you're wasting an incredible talent by hiding out here with your fabric painting when you could be working with me. It may not be as prestigious as what you did before, but I can promise you a lot of great, and fun, benefits." The moment he spoke the words and saw her frozen expression, he knew he'd committed a grave error.

"I thought after what I'd told you earlier you'd understand my feelings about business." Her quiet voice was more cutting than any sarcasm could have been. She reached down for her glasses and purse.

Before Ben could frame any kind of explanation, she was gone. He looked down at the notepad filled with her jottings. He carried the glasses back to the bar and stared at his reflection in the mirror that hung behind the glass and chrome.

"You know, mate, you really should think

before you open your big mouth. You wouldn't get into so much trouble that way," he muttered, turning away.

"That guy over at the bar says he wants to buy you a drink." Del planted himself in front of Kelly's table.

She looked up, then across the room in the direction Del was inclining his head toward. A man dressed in white slacks and a wild lime-green silk shirt nodded and smiled at her while holding up his glass in silent invitation. "I'm amazed people aren't blinded by that shirt," she muttered. "Did you tell him I don't accept drinks from anyone?"

He nodded. "I told him you're the owner and you don't drink. He still wanted me to come over and ask you if you would have a drink with him. He's talking about customer relations and that kind of crock. He wanted to come over here and talk to you himself, but I told him it wouldn't be a good idea." His expression boded ill for the man. "That's why I came over."

Kelly bit her lip to keep from smiling. "Del, you're better protection than a rottweiler. Do me a favor, thank him and explain I'm here to

work"—she tapped the ledger in front of her—
"not to socialize."

Del nodded and walked back to the bar.
Whatever he said to Kelly's newest customer
wiped the oily smile off his face. He glared at
Kelly and spun on his seat to face the bar.

"Men," she muttered, returning to her
paperwork and promptly losing herself in
deciphering Del's scrawl.

"Will my sex be forgiven if I get down on
my knees and apologize for what I said? I'm
not above groveling if it will help my case."

Kelly slid her pen through her fingers
before putting it down. "Go ahead, grovel.
Watching a man beg would really make my
day."

Ben flipped the chair around and sat down,
resting his arms across the back. "I'd crawl, but
I have a bad back." He looked around. "Busy
night."

"The regulars at Cap'n Jack's weekly poker
game usually stop by here first for a few beers
to fortify themselves." Kelly leaned forward to
confide, "Jack likes to serve his special home
brew at the games. The kindest thing to say
about it is that it removes heavy layers of paint
with ease."

"Hey, buddy, don'tcha know? The lady doesn't like to be bothered." The words rang across the room. "Her watchdog told me so."

Ben glanced toward the bar. "An admirer?"

Kelly grimaced. "One of the unfortunate side effects of the business." She waited until she caught Del's attention and inclined her head in the man's direction.

Ben watched with interest as Del approached the man and said something that apparently angered him. The man set his glass down on the bar so violently it should have shattered. He stood up and started for the door, then veered off toward Kelly.

Kelly looked up and muttered a few unlady-like words under her breath.

"Impressive vocabulary," Ben complimented.

"In a place like this, it helps." She sat back in her chair and watched the man approach her.

"Think you're something hot, don'tcha?" he sneered, swaying slightly from side to side. "Think you're too good to drink with me, but you'll talk to this bum. Lady, I make more money in six months than you'll ever see in a year. This guy"—he pointed a thumb in Ben's direction—"probably doesn't have a dime to his name."

Ben stood up. "Look, friend, you were asked to leave."

"Oh, great, an Aussie. Ever since Mel Gibson became famous you guys are a pain in the butt to us guys trying to make a good impression."

"Get out and don't come back," Kelly quietly ordered.

"Look at him, he's a bum!"

Ben looked down at his no-longer new shirt and his worn denim cutoffs. *A bum?* he mouthed to Kelly.

"Okay, you're out." Del appeared behind the man and took his arm. When the man shrugged him off, Del wrapped a beefy arm around his chest and squeezed just enough to turn his face purple.

"Get your hands off me!" The man slipped free and half turned, swinging wildly with his fist, but Del ducked and the fist connected with an unsuspecting fisherman who'd walked up to see what was going on. The fisherman reacted by throwing a punch at the man, except he hit Ben instead.

"Oh no, not again," Kelly moaned, smart enough to get out of the way and keep a chair between herself and the brawl—which, she noticed, Ben was happily participating in.

It was a long ten minutes before Harry Innes, the town's constable, and his two deputies arrived to help calm things down.

"How did it start, Miss Andrews?" Harry asked once the brawlers had been subdued and hauled off to jail—Ben among them.

She shook her head. "It was like something out of a John Wayne movie. One tries to hit a particular person but hits someone else by mistake, who retaliates and also hits the wrong person. After that, apparently, there's no way to stop it." She looked around at the turned-over tables and chairs, the broken bottles and glasses, the shattered mirror. "If that idiot who started the whole thing will pay for damages I won't press charges."

Harry nodded as he made notes. "And if he refuses?"

"Then he can be your guest as long as you like. I will be over to bail out my bartender, though. You know how Del is with his claustrophobia." She picked up her scattered ledgers and dropped them in her briefcase before closing and locking it.

"What about Mr. Wyatt?"

Kelly sighed. "What about him?"

"Are you going to bail him out too? He didn't look too good when he was taken out of here."

"The last I heard a black eye isn't life-threatening." She grimaced under the man's knowing look. She should have known the entire island was speculating about her and Ben. She finally sighed and said, "I'll think about it."

Harry chuckled. "Just be glad this doesn't happen every night." He pocketed his note-book. "I know I am."

"Come to the islands, where it's quiet and relaxing," Kelly said to Harry as she walked out the front door with him. "Guess I won't need a sign telling everyone the bar will be closed for a few days," she commented as she locked the door. "By now, everyone probably knows what happened, and some are undoubt-edly heading for the jail to bail friends and relatives out. Oh, well, it gives people some-thing to talk about for a while."

"If you're hoping they'll talk about the fight instead of you and Ben Wyatt, you're forgetting what's important around here." Harry grinned as he moved on. "I think Lili's going to start taking bets as to when Mr. Wyatt will win the lady of his choice, who just happens to be you."

"I wish you were an elected official so I could refuse to vote for you in the next election," she called after him.

Feeling more than a little disgruntled after Harry's remarks, Kelly took her time walking to the jail. Once there, it took little time to bail Del out. The stocky man lumbered out of the building, looking decidedly sheepish.

"It's as much my fault as the other guy's," he growled. "I shoulda known he'd try somethin' like that."

"It's not the first time, and we both know it won't be the last," she assured him. "We'll start cleaning up tomorrow, okay?"

He nodded. "Ya know, that Wyatt guy did real good in the fight. He wasn't afraid one bit of getting hit."

"Del."

"Yeah?"

"You say one more word about Ben Wyatt and you're fired."

He grinned, not even slightly deterred by her threat. "While we were in the holding cell, he told that guy that if he tried to come near you again he'd personally break all his bones."

Kelly stalked off. "I should have let you just suffer in there!"

"Mr. Wyatt said if you wouldn't bail me out, he would."

"Keep talking and you can go back in and let him do just that," she called over her shoulder.

"You heading home?" Del asked.

"Considering the evening I've had, it's the most logical thing to do."

By the time Kelly crossed her front threshold, her muscles were coiled tighter than springs. She dropped her purse and briefcase onto a chair and went into the kitchen for something to drink. When she walked onto the lanai, she wasn't surprised to find Ben already there, stretched out on the chaise longue.

"Do you want some ice for that eye?" she said, gesturing toward skin that was rapidly turning black and blue. "I don't have any steak to offer."

"No thanks, it's not swollen, just turning colors. I've got to hand it to you, Kelly, you sure know how to show a guy a good time. I can't remember the last time I've had so much excitement in one day."

"Luckily, that kind of excitement doesn't happen very often," she said, sinking down in a nearby chair and unscrewing the top to a bottle of wine cooler. "He was a drunken idiot who thought the price of a drink allowed him a few extra privileges. He's going to discover that price can turn out to be pretty high."

"How high?"

"I told the constable that if he pays the damages I won't press charges." She sipped her wine cooler.

Ben winced, then groaned as pain shot across the top of his face. Kelly looked sympathetic.

"I'm sorry you got in the middle of it," she said.

"Groveling might be easier on the body, but not as much fun." He took the bottle out of her fingers and drank thirstily.

"I have more inside if you'd like some of your own."

"No thanks, yours tastes better."

Kelly tucked her feet up under her body as she studied Ben. He was more rugged than the men she was used to, rougher—not just in looks, but also in temperament. So why was she so attracted to him? Because he wasn't like anyone else she'd ever known, or because she was just plain lonely for a man's company?

Something told her it was a lot more involved than either of those explanations.

"Stay for dinner," she said simply.

Ben looked up, surprised, but very delighted, by her impulsive invitation. "I'd like that."

She didn't turn away from his searching gaze. "So would I."

SEVEN

"Here, make yourself useful instead of pretending to be part of the furniture. Set the table while I get the food together." Kelly plopped plates and silverware into Ben's waiting hands. "There's a nice chardonnay in the refrigerator if you'll do the honors. I have very bad luck with wine bottle corks. Somehow I tend to pulverize them until they're nothing more than specks floating in the wine. It makes it look very unappetizing."

"And you think I can do better?" He carried everything out to the table on the lanai and soon had it properly set, complete with colorful place mats and napkins.

"Of course you can. It's in the genetic makeup of men that they can properly open wine and champagne bottles." Laughter laced her voice as she popped swordfish steaks under the broiler and began making up a pasta salad.

"Female chauvinist!" he teased.

"Of the first order and proud of it," she sang out. "Hey, you men have all the fun. Everyone knows a man's job is to clean the rain gutters, take out the trash, put up the Christmas lights, mow the lawn, all that good stuff, while we women have to battle the vacuum cleaner and ply the mop." She rummaged through a drawer, withdrew a corkscrew with a flourish, and handed it to him.

"Talk about first-class chauvinism! And you complain because we want our women barefoot and pregnant and working in the kitchen, but you have us suffering hay fever as we mow the lawn and trim the bushes."

Ben's comment, meant to be teasing, hung between them, not heavy but thoughtful, as they stared at each other for several long moments. Kelly was the first one to turn away, silently using the excuse of checking the fish.

"Why don't you go ahead and pour the wine," she suggested, purposely keeping her voice light but still looking away. "The glasses are in the cabinet to your right. Everything else will be ready in just a few moments."

Ben could have cared less when they ate. He really wanted to probe what had just happened. He wanted Kelly to talk to him, to tell him what was really on her mind. Except, he easily read the closed expression on her face. He would let things rest between them, for now.

"Since I arrived here, I find myself eating more fish than I ever have before, which is surprising, since I was never all that fond of fish before," Kelly explained, squeezing lemon juice over her share of broiled swordfish. "I guess it's because you can purchase it right off the boat here and it tastes so much better when it's very fresh."

"L.A. isn't exactly in the middle of the desert," Ben pointed out. "In fact, it has fish markets right on the water, doesn't it?"

"True, but back there it's pretty much a hassle to go down to the docks just for fish, and even then it's not the same as it is here. You may as well eat it in a restaurant." She toyed with her wine glass. "Here, you know the fishermen personally and bargaining is part of the fun of making a purchase. In L.A., your work and life have to be taken very seriously.

There's no time for just enjoying yourself. After awhile, it gets to be a bit tiring." She stared down at her plate as she moved her food around the rim.

"It sounds as if you burned out," he said. "It happens to a lot of people in the position you held. Between your work and your personal life being shot to pieces all at the same time, you were lucky to escape with your sanity intact."

Kelly looked up, her eyes narrowed. "Something tells me you did some additional checking up on me." Her soft voice was chilling. "Did what you uncover jibe with what I'd already told you?"

"I was curious, and I asked someone to fill in the blanks I figured you wouldn't tell me about." He looked down at the piece of fish his fork had just impaled and knew just how that fish felt.

"And?"

"And, you had an impeccable business reputation, ran a tight ship, didn't believe in taking prisoners, and never said a word nor made a promise you couldn't back up. No businessman worth his salt allowed your lovely face to sway him, because it was a good way to lose," he stated. "There are some who feel the only mistake you made was with your marriage, but they put that down to being just one of those things. Your ex-husband tried to claim he was due more than half of your marital assets by insisting he helped you set up some of your business deals and introduced you to a lot of influential people, but I understand that he was the one to inhabit the Hollywood social set, not you. The trouble is, his mouth went too far; he couldn't back his statements up. But in the end you still gave him more than he deserved, because you just wanted him out of your life. I am curious about one thing: Did you really punch him in the face on the courthouse steps? And then hit his lawyer?"

Kelly nodded. "If you want to really upset an actor you bruise his most valuable asset, his face. Plus I ruined some very expensive dental work. I'd never understood the satisfaction a man gets from hitting another man until then. My hand hurt for hours afterward and my knuckles were bruised, but it was worth it." She picked up her glass and sipped her wine. "I wouldn't hesitate doing it again if I felt it was necessary. I don't like being checked up on, Mr. Wyatt. If you want to know something, ask me. If I refuse to answer it's because I don't consider it relevant to our dealings."

"What you really mean is it wouldn't be any of my business."

Her smile didn't quite reach her eyes. "That's another way of putting it."

Ben leaned back in his chair. "I didn't exactly ask for a written report about you, Kelly. What I learned was nothing more than public knowledge. I will admit you do intrigue me. You're very plainspoken, which is unusual in the business world, where most people like to evade anything that smacks of the truth. I'm used to people saying one thing and meaning another. I'm sure you've encountered it a time or two."

"Much more than a time or two, but that didn't mean I liked it. It doesn't matter anymore, since I no longer have to participate in it. My "dress for success" clothing now belongs to someone else, I sold my Jag, and I gave my ex the house. I'm now doing something purely for myself, and I'm very happy with the person I've become and with what I do. That's all that matters."

"Even though essentially you ran away from your old life."

Her head snapped up at his soft-spoken taunt. "I didn't run away from anything."

Ben's fingers curled around the wineglass

stem. "You ran away because you couldn't handle facing the truth. You were afraid, Kelly."

Her cheekbones stretched taut with suppressed fury. "I have never been afraid of anything." She stressed each word, her eyes glinting golden lights.

"You're afraid of things you can't control," he gently pressed. "You decided if you weren't there nothing bad could happen to you and no one would learn you have a vulnerable side."

Her hands, lying on top of the table, balled into fists. "I told you, I didn't want anyone's pity!"

"It wasn't pity you were afraid of. It was the idea that people would care about what happened to you—and that some wouldn't. You found it easier to escape than to find out who your friends truly were in your time of need. What you did wasn't wrong, Kelly. And I can't say I'm not happy that you did run away." He reached across the table and covered her hand with his. Her skin was ice cold under his touch. "I'm just glad you stopped running when you arrived here. Otherwise, I might not have met you. Perhaps we could call it fate working in our favor."

"Fate is a word, nothing more."

"I used to think that way. Not anymore.

Especially now, when it seems everyone on the island is watching us to see what will happen, and hoping for the best."

"It's because they all feel everyone should be in love. Too many French citizens settled here. It's well known that love is a major part of their lifestyle." Her lips twitched.

Ben rose from the table and walked around to Kelly's chair. With a twist of his wrist, he had her on her feet and guided her reluctant body toward the edge of the lanai, where a chaise longue had a perfect view of the ocean. He sat and pulled her down until she curled up against him.

"The dishes." She shifted her body into a more comfortable position even as she feebly protested.

"They're not going anywhere." He cupped the back of her head, pressing it against his chest. "We've had a busy day and deserve a few minutes of peace and quiet. Besides, I like holding you."

She turned her head so she could look into his face. In the moonlight, his features looked like sharply etched silver. "You don't back down from anything, do you?"

His smile warmed her. "No, I don't. Call it Aussie stubbornness. It used to get me in a lot of fights in school. My mother was an expert in patching up cuts and scrapes and treating black eyes. She never scolded me for coming home with torn clothes. She just hugged me and told me she was proud of my willingness to stand up for myself. She also suggested I take some boxing lessons."

"Your mother sounds wonderful. Very supportive."

"She is. She's the real backbone of the family." Ben wrapped his arms around Kelly in a warm embrace. "You'll like her."

"You also take too much for granted." She closed her eyes. "Pushy man."

"Another point for my side! This time you said it affectionately." He dropped a kiss on her brow, then another just under her left eye. "I'm getting to you, aren't I?"

"Like a cold virus," she retorted, but there was no resentment in her voice. There couldn't be with the smile curving her lips. She couldn't remember the last time she had felt so relaxed with a man. The idea of having a man treat her so lovingly was still new to her. "Michael believed all he had to do was smile at a woman and she'd fall into his arms. He figured the sight of his manly chest and flashing white teeth would make up for the fact that he wasn't all that great in bed." She giggled suddenly. "I can't believe I said that! I must have had more wine than I thought."

His arms tightened around her. "Thanks for letting me know, in your own way, that he never satisfied you."

Kelly shifted around until she lay over him, with her arms crossed in front of her and her chin resting atop them on his chest. "While I'm known for speaking bluntly, that's usually a subject I leave alone. I'm not bitter, and I'm not still in love with him, probably because I don't think I ever was in love with him. I think I just felt it was time to settle down, and at the time he was the likeliest prospect. There was lust involved, but not love, which made it a losing proposition from the beginning. The divorce proceedings lasted longer than the marriage did. No wonder I needed to get away from everything."

He ran his palm slowly up and down her back, feeling her body start to lose its tension within seconds. "I had a talk with my legal department and with the hotel manager today. The contract will have a few revisions before I sign, thanks to you."

"What can I say? I'm a genius. Tell me about your home," she said in a sleepy voice.

"Which one? I have a very nice house in Sydney that overlooks the water. It's mostly glass, very modern, has everything a person could need. Then I have another place in the outback with sheep and horses and the chance to ride wherever I want without running into another human being," he told her, still moving his hands up and down her back in a slow caress. He wondered how long he had before going insane with her weight—and her loveliness—on him.

"Does your ranch have a flower garden?"

"It takes someone out there all the time to work with flowers and I'm out there only when I have a few free days, which isn't as often as I'd like," he explained. "But I'm planning on retiring out there."

"That's one of the first things I loved here. All the flowers so lush and sweet-smelling. And the way people took the time to just enjoy life. No rushing off to meetings or power lunches. No worrying about whether you'll get that promotion by your personal target date and who you'll have to walk over for it. I basically inherited part of my financial company when my dad died, but I still had to prove I could do the job, and the only way to do that was to work harder than anyone else. Women still aren't allowed to show any weakness. I couldn't have headaches, PMS, or a generally bad day." She laughed huskily. "No wonder I was so worn out when I came here."

"And now you're a new woman. One who wears casual clothing with ease and swims nude in the ocean late at night without worrying about an audience. Who paints her dreams on fabric to share with others."

She raised her head enough to graze his chin with her lips. The sandpaper roughness of his skin teased her senses; the salty taste invited her to partake of more. Even though she had been known to be aggressive in business, Kelly wasn't used to being the aggressor with a man. But this time was different, because she could feel Ben silently urging her on. She used her fingertips to trace random patterns on his chest. She rubbed his nipple through his shirt, watching the tiny nub raise up. Needing to touch his bare skin, she slipped the buttons free and parted his shirt.

"Your skin is always so warm," she whispered, placing her palm against his chest, feeling the crisp hair prick her skin. She noted the change in his respiration as she moved her palm in a lazy circle over his abdomen. "It's as if you have an internal solar unit that stores it up."

"More likely it has something to do with you, love," he rasped. "You're getting me all hot and bothered."

"Am I?" Her lips followed the path her hand had taken.

"You know you are."

"Are you complaining?"

"Only if you stop what you're doing." He grasped her shoulders, pulling her upward until she faced him. His hopes soared when he saw the laughter dancing in her eyes. The lady was obviously loosening up. "I hope you realize that I'm not just a plaything you can toy with, then toss aside like a worn-out shoe."

"You needn't worry. I promise to always respect you," she purred, scratching his bare chest with her fingernails.

"That's good to know, because I will expect you to do the right thing by me," he continued in his deceptively soft voice, its slightly harsh accent grating pleasantly on her ears. "That means a large family, say four or six. I always did prefer even numbers."

"Six?" Her gasp exploded into laughter. "That's fifty-four months of pregnancy!"

"Of course, there will be time off between

children. Just to give us some breathing room," he continued.

"How generous of you." Her sarcasm wasn't lost on him.

"One of the guest bedrooms has excellent light, so we could easily fix it up into a workroom for you," he went on, not entirely oblivious to her not-too-subtle attempts to drive him crazy by moving her hips against his in a seductive circle. He suddenly wished there weren't any clothing between them. "There would be no problem in installing a skylight if you'd like one."

"You're being presumptuous again," she warned without heat in her voice. "You never stop, do you?" Surprisingly, she knew she really didn't want him to. Being pursued as Kelly, the woman, was new to her. And she liked it.

"I believe in planning ahead." Ben moved so swiftly Kelly didn't realize his intention, until she found herself sprawled on the chaise with him on top of her, his hips neatly fitting inside her feminine cradle, his elbows placed next to her shoulders. "Besides, since you're obviously not the type to give in easily, I'll just have to keep trying to prove to you what a wonderful catch I am and that you can't live without me. I'm even willing to be your sex slave." His grin flashed white.

Her fingers found their way into the silky strands lying against his nape. "Um, your idea sounds awfully kinky," she murmured. "And interesting. Do you also indulge in silk scarves and feathers when you're a woman's sex slave?"

"I'm not usually willing to bow under a woman's will, but you could probably persuade me to try anything," he whispered in her ear as he nibbled her earlobe. "As long as you're the one who has the scarves and feathers. Or you could tie me to the bed with silk scarves and wear nothing but feathers while you're driving me crazy. I wouldn't mind."

"Feathers make me sneeze. I'd have to look into something else to tantalize you with."

"I'd like that." He nuzzled that soft spot just behind her ear. "What else would you do to drive me crazy? Wear a garter belt, stockings, high heels, and nothing else? I always thought those black fishnet stockings French maids wear with those short skirts were very sexy."

"I don't recall any of the French maids I've seen wearing fishnet stockings, much less short skirts," she countered, enjoying this light sexual banter. "Although there was a play I attended a few years ago that had a French maid wearing such an outfit."

"You never saw one outside of a play and you claim you lived in California?" he teased, biting down gently on her earlobe. "I would think sexy little French maids were mandatory out there."

Her air supply was turning out to be very limited and she felt weak in the knees. She was grateful she was lying down. "Yes, well, I never got out much except for business functions."

"You've led a deprived life, Kelly. Business functions are only useful in one way. Otherwise, you might as well have visited your dentist for a root canal."

A slight frown creased her forehead as something occurred to her. "Considering how important you must consider it, what with time limits and such, I'm surprised you haven't talked about your new boutique once tonight."

Her comment surprised him. "Was I supposed to?"

She shrugged. "Well, you do have a meeting with the hotel's manager and the owner tomorrow to finalize the contract. I would have thought that's all you'd want to talk about."

Ben levered back. Anger warred with confusion on his face. "I'm on a tropical island with a lovely woman in my arms and you think I'm going to talk business? There is no way I would allow all this romantic moonlight or these ocean breezes to go to waste. Give me some credit, Kelly. I do have priorities, and as far as I'm concerned, business is pretty far down the list right now."

She searched his features, amazed she could read his emotions so easily, as if she'd known him for a long time. Sometimes, she acknowledged, she felt as if she did. She wondered how he had gotten so far in business with such open features.

"Who says I'm so open in my business dealings?"

It wasn't until then that she realized she'd expressed her thoughts out loud. "I'm just surprised you're so easy to read, that's all."

"Maybe you're one of the few who can read me that easily," he pointed out. "And if so, there can only be a couple of reasons."

She knew she shouldn't ask, but she couldn't resist. "And what are they?"

He held up a finger. "One, because I allow you to. Two, because, as crazy as it sounds, we are two souls destined to be one." The words ended in a hushed whisper as his mouth moved closer to hers.

For one of the few times in her life, Kelly had nothing to say. She feared that he could be very right and feared that giving in to Ben the way he wanted her to, and the way she wanted to, would change her life so irrevocably she would never be the same again.

EIGHT

"Kelly can't come to the phone right now because she's asleep. At the sound of the beep, leave your name and telephone number and she might get back to you when she has a chance to wake up," Kelly mumbled into the phone that had had the horrible nerve to disturb her sleep once she'd succumbed to a deep slumber a little after dawn. "Beep."

"Do not play games, *cherie*," Lili's musical voice, filled with laughter, sang out. "I called to tell you a package arrived for you on this morning's plane. Out of my kind heart I accepted it for you."

Kelly squinted as she rolled over and tried to read the digital numbers on the bedside clock. She couldn't believe it was after ten!

She rarely slept this late. "I'm not expecting anything for at least another two weeks."

"I do not think this was something you were expecting," Lili replied. "As I said, I accepted the package for you. Please come down so I can see what it is!"

"Lili, I'm not even awake," Kelly protested, resisting the urge to pull the pillow over her face and go back to sleep. "Feel free to open the box and tell me what it is, if you're that desperate to know. Besides, it's probably from Elaine. You remember the last time, when she sent me what looked like ten years' worth of skin preparations that turned out to be a six-month supply, all because she was convinced I'd end up with leathery skin or worse if I didn't take proper care of it. With my luck, she probably sent another six-month supply, which I will gladly hand over to you." She stifled a yawn that threatened to crack her jaw.

"I doubt this has anything to do with skin care, unless it is a special preparation that requires packing in dry ice," Lili interrupted.

Dry ice? Kelly sat up in bed. "Lili, please, I'm not up to guessing games!"

"Then get out of bed, get dressed, and come down here to see what your surprise is. I do not open other people's mail, even with their permission." Lili hung up before Kelly could say anything more.

Kelly dropped the receiver in the cradle and flopped back against the pillows. "Fat chance." With stubborn determination, she rolled over and closed her eyes. A few seconds passed before they popped open again. She uttered a curse and threw the covers back. Lili was right: She did want to know what had been sent to her. Especially something packed in dry ice. "Elaine, if it's more skin care creams, I will take the next plane to L.A. and force you to eat the contents of every jar and tube," she muttered to her faraway friend, heading for the bathroom for a much-needed wake-up shower.

It was a little more than an hour before Kelly passed through the open doorway to Lili's shop. While she'd been ready in less than a half hour, she'd deliberately taken her time over breakfast and drank several cups of coffee so she wouldn't appear overeager. There had been something in Lili's voice that teased her curiosity, but she wasn't about to rush!

"I'm glad to see you made the time to come down here for your mail," Lili greeted her, passing through the silky seashell-pink curtains that divided the storeroom from the front of the shop.

"You didn't indicate it was an emergency." Kelly forced herself to stop and inspect multitiered glass shelving displaying delicate crystal perfume bottles. "Are these new? They're lovely. I especially like this black one."

"They are not new and you know it. Come with me." Without looking back, Lili disappeared into the rear of the shop, confident Kelly would follow. "Obviously, you did not take the time to dress properly," Lili said, exaggerating her slight disapproval of Kelly's faded shorts and tank top.

"Pushy, very pushy," Kelly muttered, following the older woman.

Lili pointed to a large carton pushed into a corner of the crowded storeroom.

"I don't think this is from Elaine," Kelly pronounced, reading the address label and finding nothing to identify the sender. "Besides, she usually calls or writes to let me know she's sending something off."

"An old lover, perhaps?" Lili sat in a small velvet-cushioned chair that resided by her tiny desk.

Kelly rolled her eyes. "I doubt it. And all Michael would send me would be a court summons." She studied the carton's lettering. "Why the dry ice?"

Lili leaned forward and handed her a lethal-looking letter opener. "There is only one way to find out."

Kelly carefully slit the packing tape and opened the box, folding back the lid. A squeal of delight escaped her lips as she looked inside. "I can't believe it! And the dry ice was used so they wouldn't melt." She pulled out a box, then another, before pausing long enough to open one of the boxes and retrieve an object wrapped in silver plastic. She rapidly tore it open and bit into the chewy chocolate confection.

Lili looked horrified. "Candy for breakfast?"

"Not just candy—Goo Goo Clusters!" Kelly's voice was muffled by the caramel and marshmallow filling. "This is my all-time favorite candy." She stopped. "And very few people know about it." She looked at it with wonder. "This is more romantic than flowers." she murmured, raising her head. "Ben knows how much I love these, and he somehow took the time to find them and have them shipped to me, without any indication they were sent by him. Don't you see?"

Lili's smile filled her narrow features. "I am a woman. Of course I see. And I'm glad to see that you do also."

"He could have sent me flowers by the dozen, but they wouldn't have meant a thing, because flowers are all over this island. And fancy chocolates aren't my style. But this isn't something you can just find in any store," she explained.

"If I didn't know better, I would say you are in love with him."

Kelly's hand froze in the process of lifting the rest of the candy to her mouth. "Oh, no. That's one word I refuse to discuss." She held up her hands as if warding off the devil. In her eyes, they were one and the same. She hurriedly repacked the candy boxes and picked up the unwieldy carton. "Thank you for keeping this for me. I'd leave some as payment, but I'm afraid this is one thing I don't share. Stop by the house later and I'll let you have one of the new T-shirts I designed with pastels depicting a waterfall scene." She knew better than to confide the fact that the idea came to her after that morning picnic with Ben. Lili would try to make entirely too much of it. Just as she was doing now.

Kelly somehow made it out to her Jeep with the carton, then carefully set it in the passenger seat. Lili followed her outside. "I do not care what you say. I only know what I see. The two of you will make beautiful children," she called after Kelly. "And I want to be their godmother."

Kelly gunned the engine so hard she feared she might over-rev it. "Don't hold your breath!" she yelled as she roared down the road.

Lili didn't stop smiling. "We will see," she murmured, returning to her shop.

Kelly hurriedly stowed her treasures in the refrigerator before snatching up the phone. Her call to the hotel told her that Mr. Wyatt was in a business meeting. She left a message for him as she told herself it was just as well.

"To work, lady," she ordered herself, heading for her workroom. "After all, you have a contract and deadlines to uphold."

It didn't take her long to lose herself in an array of shimmering pastel paints as she began feathering a new design onto a butter-colored T-shirt with a broad brush covered with bronze paint. She hummed along to some soft-rock golden oldies, her hips swaying to the beat drifting from her CD player as she worked.

Kelly lost all concept of time as she worked on her new designs, every once in a while stepping back to admire her handiwork.

"You do great work, Andrews," she figuratively patted herself on the back.

"That's what I've always said."

Kelly spun around to find Ben standing on the other side of the closed screen door leading to the beach.

"I rang the bell, but I guess you didn't hear it!" he explained. "At first I thought you weren't home, but then I heard the music and thought I'd take a chance."

She gestured. "Come in and see what masterpieces I'm creating for your shops. If I do say so myself, this is my best work yet."

Ben entered the room and looked around at the T-shirts and beach cover-ups hung around the room. Most only had the lines of the transferred pattern on them, with only a few already painted. This time, there were no beach scenes, no tropical air to the designs. All were more free-form, geometric, in either glittering pastel shades or brilliant jewel tones.

He examined the butter-colored shirt Kelly had begun her work session with, examining the slashes of bronze, gold, and pewter across the front.

"These are incredible," he murmured, fingering the T-shirt's sleeve hem, which had been decorated with tiny copper stars. "Very bold, exciting, sensual." He lifted his head, and his eyes captured hers with hot eloquence. "Like their creator."

She didn't veer from his gaze. Whatever made her think she could deny herself a man who made her feel the way he did? Why did she even bother trying when, deep down, she really didn't want to? "I wanted to do something different."

"You achieved it." He released the shirt, only to reach for her and pull her toward him. "And more."

Kelly's arms easily found their natural place around his neck where her fingers could entangle themselves in the silky strands lying against his nape. "Then you like what you see?" she asked throatily and with a saucy wiggle of her hips that instantly aroused him.

His hands rested against her waist. "More than like. Much more. But then, you've known that from the beginning. Sweetheart, if you keep it up, you're going to have more than you bargained for."

She stopped wiggling but didn't move from her spot, where her hips lightly grazed his. She tipped her head back. "Did I thank you for my Goo Goo Clusters?"

"Not yet."

"Then I thank you now. You really know how to get to a lady's heart, Mr. Wyatt. I ate my last one about two months ago, so they were a wonderful surprise."

"Somehow, I sensed you would appreciate them more than flowers or a box of traditional candy." He dipped his head, inhaling the light fragrance emanating from her skin. Faint iridescent sparkles dusted glittering lights along her throat and chest area, bared by her scoop-necked tank top. A delicate gold filigree chain rested just above the hollow in her throat. "Did you know your skin is shining like moonlight right now? Tell me, do you smell this wonderful all over?" he murmured, entranced by the light display dancing across her tanned skin.

"It's the body lotion I use. It's wickedly expensive, but I feel I'm worth it." Laughter hovered on her lips, laughter Ben had to share in the best way possible. His mouth covered hers in a light but telltale kiss.

"I'll have to make a note of the name and buy you a case of it," he breathed against her parted lips.

Kelly stepped back just enough to break the spell. "The candy, you can buy all you want. The body lotion I can purchase all on my own," she said softly but firmly.

He was fast becoming an expert at knowing when to back off from her. "Moving too fast again?"

"No, I just have my own code, and there are some things I don't appreciate a man buying for me, as if they're buying my favors."

Ben smiled, taking no offense at her words. He knew, only too well, just how independent Kelly was and that she wasn't a woman to be wooed with gifts. "My sweet lady, I doubt a truckload of diamonds and emeralds could sway your affections. Although I did have a few hopes the chocolate would speak for me." He grinned.

"The man has style," she declared. "But you may be wrong—a truckload of diamonds and emeralds probably *could* sway me a little," she mused, tipping her head to one side. Her ponytail swung over her shoulder, resting against her skin in a natural curl. "Just a little, mind you, but don't let me hold you back if you feel the need to try."

The "need" Ben felt at that moment was to carry her off to the nearest bed. He drew in several deep breaths. "I thought we could take a picnic lunch over to the other side of the island and go swimming."

Her eyes lit up with joy at the idea, then just as quickly dimmed. "I have so much work still to do," she murmured, glancing around the room. "I usually set out to finish a certain number of items in a given time period, and I'm a bit behind. It sounds wonderful, Ben, but I just can't. Not today."

"Even if I say I don't mind if some of the merchandise is late?" he tempted. "I've never thought of myself as a slave driver."

She slowly shook her head. "It's not the way I do business. While I may live on a tropical island that has its own special time zone, I still adhere to a more conventional one. But we could negotiate a compromise."

His hopes soared. "I'm amiable," he said casually.

"A picnic dinner instead of picnic lunch. I'll provide the dinner if you'll provide the wine."

Dinner, darkness, perhaps a little moonlight . . . Yes, he could see the advantages in that. "What time shall I return to pick you up?"

Kelly looked around again, gauging how much more she wanted to do before the end of her workday and adding in some extra time to clean up. "Make it about seven," she said, splaying her hands against his chest and using them to gently push him out of the room. "Now go and let me get back to work, so I'll be finished in time!"

Ben stole just enough time to kiss her thoroughly before leaving. Once he was out of sight, Kelly leaned against the worktable, holding on tightly before her jellied knees gave out.

"Whew!" She fanned herself with her hand. "I think I just learned what a hot flash is like. The man is positively lethal." Her lips curved. "Now I guess I'll just have to show him it can work two ways."

Ben believed punctuality was a virtue, especially when a beautiful woman was involved. He stood on Kelly's doorstep two minutes to seven, wondering if he'd ever felt this impatient when he was a teenager, and doubting it.

"Are you coming inside or aren't you ready to wake up yet?" Kelly's laughing voice startled him. "Our dinner, as promised." She pushed a wicker picnic basket against his chest, then pulled the door closed behind her as she stepped outside. "Am I to believe you had to wait so long for me to answer the door that you fell into a trance?"

He grimaced. "I guess you could say I was thinking back to my misspent youth," he admitted, "wondering if I'd ever been this impatient before when picking up a date."

"And?"

"And I doubt it, since I didn't know any girls like you then." He looked over her cotton strapless dress of rich brown and cream tones with swirls of cinnamon in the full skirt. She had twisted her hair up in a loose knot with tortoiseshell chopsticks sticking out of it, in the kind of style any red-blooded man would itch to take down. And Ben's blood was about as red as you could get. He grasped her hand, weaving his fingers between hers, while his other hand held on to the picnic basket as they walked toward the Jeep.

"You wouldn't have *wanted* to know me then," she pronounced. "I was pretty gawky during my teen years," she told him as he helped her into the Jeep. "I was all knees and elbows, wore braces, and thought zit cream was my best friend. I hate to think what would have happened to me if my mother hadn't enrolled me in a charm course with instructors who showed tall, gangly girls like me that there were swans deep inside us ugly ducklings."

Ben slid behind the wheel. "I can't imagine you ever feeling insecure. From the first moment I laid eyes on you I saw a self-assured woman who wouldn't allow anyone to get in her way."

Kelly laughed as she shook her head. "Now, yes. Back then, anything but. I was the only girl who was taller than most of the boys in my class and was always tripping over my own two big feet. I was saved by a wonderful instructor at the charm school who showed me how to walk without tripping and that standing tall wasn't such a bad thing—especially when there were boys around who were taller than myself. My parents used to tell me I'd grow into my height, but I thought they were just saying it because I was their daughter. It took some time to realize they meant it. Later on, working in my dad's office helped." She suddenly looked uncomfortable.

"I'm sure you didn't expect me to ramble on like this."

He placed his hand over hers. "How else will we learn about each other if we don't ramble on? Believe me, the time will come when I talk about some of my less-than-admirable deeds."

"Such as?" she prompted, as he knew she would.

He switched on the engine and put the Jeep in gear. "Such as the time I was ten and let my uncle's stallion out into the paddock with his prize mares."

Kelly's mouth dropped open. She wasn't sure whether to laugh or act shocked. "Oh, no!"

"Oh, yes. My dad made sure I didn't sit down for a while," he said ruefully. "I didn't try anything like that again. I cleaned all the stalls in the mares' barns by myself for the rest of my visit, which stretched into the entire school holiday. I couldn't look at a horse again for almost a year, but I ended up with great muscles."

"Which I'm sure all the girls adored," Kelly commented, pausing to point to what looked like nothing more than a dirt path. "Take that road. It's pretty bumpy and has a lot of potholes, since it isn't used a lot, but it leads to a nice stretch of beach that's one of the island's best-kept secrets."

Ben peered through the windshield. "Are you sure that's a road?"

"Don't be so skeptical. I told you: It's an island secret not revealed to tourists."

Ben let out a laugh coupled with a groan when the Jeep hit the first pothole. His hands tightened on the steering wheel. "Are you sure it's worth it?" he shouted.

She grabbed hold of the dashboard to keep her balance. "You'll see soon enough."

The Jeep was jostled right and left, bouncing its passengers, as Ben tried to steer around the holes in the road.

"No beach is worth this," he grumbled, slowing down when the road seemed to just disappear in front of him.

"Oh, yes it is." Kelly climbed out and gestured ahead. "Go take a look and tell me some bruises on your rear end aren't worth what you're seeing out there."

Ben walked in the direction she was pointing. He realized the road dead-ended onto the sand as he walked a bit farther and found nothing but a lengthy stretch of sand, with the sound of rolling waves beyond that.

"Well, what do you think? Was all the bouncing around worth it?" Kelly asked from behind.

He didn't turn around. He just took in the scene before him, a scene he'd viewed once before—on the canvas tote bag his mother used when she went shopping. As many times as he'd admired the work—Kelly's work—he had no idea it was real until now.

"Oh yes," he breathed. "More than worth it."

NINE

Without taking his eyes off the picture-postcard view in front of him, Ben reached down and pulled off his deck shoes. "I guess no one would complain if we left our shoes here." He dropped them on the sand's edge.

"There's been no complaints so far, probably because the island gremlins go to bed at dusk." She walked toward him, carrying a blanket. "I didn't want you to feel left out, so I left the basket and wine in the Jeep for you to get out."

He was reluctant to leave the idyllic scene before him. "Okay," he murmured, before slowly turning around to head back to the vehicle.

By the time he returned with the basket

and the wine bottles in a mesh bag slung over his shoulder, Kelly was kneeling in the middle of the blanket, smoothing out the edges. She looked up with a bright smile when Ben set down the basket and bag.

"I may not cook as well as the resort's chef," she told him as she opened the basket and set out various tidbits, "but you won't starve either. I figured our best bet would be finger food."

"I already learned that the day you served that excellent Mexican meal," he said, dropping down beside her.

They sat cross-legged across from each other, pulling vegetables out of containers and coating the ends with an herbal dip.

"Is this a hint I'm eating too much rich food?" Ben held up a celery stick before dunking it in the herbal dip and chewing off the end.

"I've been eating too much junk food lately, and I can't imagine you've been a good boy dining on broiled fish since you've arrived when the chef can conjure up those wonderful sauces that taste so good because they're ninety-nine percent butter. So tonight, we'll feast on food that's good for us." Kelly stretched out on her side, bracing herself up on one elbow. "So, tell me, are you all signed, sealed, and delivered on your shop space?"

He nodded as he reached for the mesh bag and opened the wine bottle with a brisk efficiency Kelly admired. "It's now ironclad. For once no one's wasting any time, because the boutique has been badly needed in the hotel ever since the other one closed. I guess they hadn't found a suitable replacement until I came on the scene," he said without a trace of arrogance. Ben knew his shops sold a quality product, but he didn't believe in broadcasting the fact—he preferred that his sales personnel do that. "Some walls are being painted tomorrow and wallpaper will be put up on the others soon after that."

Kelly suddenly felt an awful uneasiness in her stomach. If the shop's interior moved along swiftly, it meant Ben would leave that much sooner. She reminded herself that he could even leave now if he wanted to, since the contract was taken care of.

"And I'll be interviewing applicants for the manager's position and making sure the merchandise is received in time for the shop's opening," he explained, seeming oblivious to Kelly's tension.

Her jaws ached from grinding her teeth. "And?"

He poured wine into two shallow plastic cups. "And when it's all finished I'll be back in my office wishing I could spend more evenings on the beach with a beautiful woman."

Kelly rotated the cup between her palms. Considering how warm the evening was, she felt very cold.

"Amazing how quickly things can happen once the ball starts rolling," she murmured. "I guess I did a much better job with your contract than I thought I did. One can be too good at their job, I guess. Perhaps I should have let a few points remain open for bargaining purposes."

"I guess you've never met Rene, the resort's owner," Ben explained. "He's one of those rare Frenchmen who doesn't include the word "bargaining" in his vocabulary. He believes every business deal is cut-and-dried, that his contracts are perfect and not to be questioned."

She stared at the remaining food, now not in the least bit hungry. She hated herself for feeling the way she did. She'd done well without someone to care about for a long time now, and didn't like the idea that she suddenly cared too much. "Do you have any idea when you'll return to Australia?"

"In about a week or so, but I'll be back for the shop's grand opening." He stretched out on his side, facing her, then picked up her free hand and laced his fingers through hers. "Will you miss me?"

She looked everywhere but at him. "It's not nice to ask leading questions like that."

"It's not nice to ignore them either." He lifted her fingers, deliberately brushing them across his slightly parted lips. "Humor me. Tell me you'll miss me like hell and you won't sleep soundly until I come back."

Kelly shifted her body so that she could hover just above his reclining figure. "I'll miss you like hell and I won't sleep soundly until you come back."

"Try it again, and put some feeling into it," he invited, enjoying the game.

Kelly dipped her head. Her lips rested a breath above his. Even in the dim evening light, he had no trouble seeing them glisten with the bronzed copper lipstick she wore.

"What do you want to hear, Wyatt?" she breathed, resting one hand on each of his shoulders, which kept her—especially from the midriff down—a tantalizing distance away.

"That you are the best thing to come into my life in a long time and I don't even want to contemplate the future without you? That you're one of the best lovers I've ever had?"

"*One* of the best?"

She went on as if he hadn't spoken. "That life will never be the same once you're gone? Get real, Wyatt. Women don't say that anymore. They just pick up the pieces and get on with their lives." She started to lever back, but Ben's hands gripped her arms and refused to release her.

"One of the best?" he repeated. "You couldn't even lie and say I was *the* best?"

Laughter danced in her eyes. "And have your ego inflate from such blatant flattery? No way."

He pulled her down on top of him so she would have no doubt it wasn't his ego that was inflated. "Humor me."

She nuzzled his ear, lips and teeth nibbling along the way. "You are one of the sexiest men alive that I've ever been lucky enough to meet. You have the hands of an artist who can stroke beautiful paintings from women, the kind of voice that sends delightful shivers down a woman's back and you . . ." She laughed softly as she paused before whispering dark, erotic words and sexy suggestions in his ear. As if that wasn't enough to send his blood pressure skyrocketing, her fingers were tap-dancing their way down his chest, only hesitating long enough to undo each button and to spread his cotton shirt enough to bare his chest until she reached the waistband of his shorts. She bypassed that for the zipper, which bulged from his erection. "Isn't it amazing the effect words can have on a person?" she marveled, drawing circles around that area.

"Kelly." The word came out in a hiss of frustration. He wrapped his fingers around her wrist, fingers that were as tension-filled as his voice.

"Shut up, Ben, and let me do this my way," she murmured as she idly played with the zipper tab before slowly lowering it.

"You're killing me!"

"Don't worry, I haven't lost a patient yet."

Kelly was quickly discovering that seducing a man was not only very enjoyable, but extremely stimulating as well. The more Ben grew aroused under her ministrations, the more aroused she grew. She found herself taking the dominant role in stride, even though she'd never done anything like this before. But with Ben it seemed right, natural.

She rubbed her nose lightly against the corner of his eye, imagining that the tiny lines that radiated outward were guiding her to new, undiscovered spots. She dropped butterfly kisses on each closed eyelid, whispering all the while how desirable she found him and how there was nothing like a tropical island for a seduction.

Ben blindly searched for the zipper on Kelly's dress and swore under his breath when he encountered only silky cotton fabric. "How do you keep this thing up?" He muttered a curse when he slid his hand up her leg and along her thigh and discovered bare skin, without any kind of covering. He was only glad he hadn't known of her lack of underwear sooner or he would have surely gone crazy.

She smiled as she brushed her lips across his, parting them enough so her tongue could slip inside. "Willpower."

Before Ben's wits could entirely desert him, he found the source of her willpower, in the form of a wide band of elastic in the back of her dress. He dragged the top down to expose her breasts. His palms covered them in a warm caress, his fingers rolling her nipples while their mouths feasted on each other. Although he wanted nothing more than to roll her over and fan the flames even brighter, he sensed it was important to Kelly to finish what she started. Not to mention he was enjoying her kisses and caresses too much. He inhaled sharply when her open mouth settled warmly on his chest, beginning a heated, damp trail across his skin, from one flat copper-colored nipple to the other, before moving slowly downward. He gripped handfuls of her hair, sending strands flying over his fingers as she reached her target. Fire shot everywhere through Ben's body. He blinked to keep the sweat out of his eyes as he fell into the abyss he'd only been tottering on the edge of until now. But it still wasn't enough for him. Gathering up the last bit of reserves in his body, he pulled her face up to his and rolled over until he lay against her body. He quickly pulled her dress down farther until it lay in a tumbled heap on the sand, along with his own clothing, which had been so hastily discarded that neither of them had any memory of who had undressed who.

The moonlight dappled their bare skin with silvery shadows as they hungrily reached for each other again and again, touching, and caressing, tasting with open mouths but always putting off that last movement, as if they wanted to prolong the ecstatic agony as long as possible. He settled his palm against the dark, springy curls at the top of her thighs before caressing her core and finding her damp and inviting. She moaned his name and shifted her legs in a silent invitation. Ben looked down at Kelly, whose open eyes stared back at him. Her head was thrown back, the cords standing out in her neck.

"Are you sure?" Even though his control was badly slipping, he felt the need to ask, to know she wanted him as much as he wanted her.

She placed her hand against his cheek. "I've been arguing with myself for too long now," she murmured, stroking the beard-roughened skin. "Instead of arguing, I should have realized that I wouldn't allow myself to get entangled in any situation guaranteed to hurt me. I want you, Ben. Very much." She caressed his heated length before guiding him into her waiting sheath. She pulsed around him, drawing him in even deeper.

Ben closed his eyes. As he had the last time, he felt as if he'd just come home. It all felt so right to him, so perfect, that he never wanted to leave. But his body didn't want to rest and savor the moment.

He touched his lips against her brow line.

"While my brain wants to take this slow and easy, my body is telling me something different."

Kelly wrapped her arms and legs around him. "This isn't a time for slow and easy, Ben. We want each other too much." Her hips moved in accompaniment to her words, silently encouraging him to soar with her—as if he needed an invitation.

Kelly's senses raced with so many sensations, she felt as if she was being torn apart in different directions. This time was nothing like that first night. Not because anticipation had grown so high since then, but because their emotions were much more involved this time. She clawed at Ben, needing to stay with him, needing to know he was still with her.

"I'm here, baby," he panted, increasing his thrusts. "I won't leave you."

Her entire body tightened until it felt like a taut violin string. She arched up, holding on as the world exploded around her. By then she was past caring, and she did something she thought she never would. She told a man she loved him while in the throes of passion.

"Did all the wine spill out on the sand?" Kelly's voice was sleepy and sated as she lay in Ben's arms.

He looked over her shoulder. "Just the bottle I opened."

She giggled, burrowing closer against his side. "The sand crabs will end up drunk."

"And healthy, since the food went every which way too." Without loosening his hold on Kelly, he reached for the second bottle, which lay in the sand next to the blanket. In the end he had to move away from Kelly's delicious form and sit up so he could pop the cork. "I should have bought a cheaper wine with a screw top," he grumbled, struggling with the corkscrew until the cork popped free. Their plastic tumblers were filled with wine-soaked sand, so he handed the bottle to her. She drank thirstily, then handed it to him and watched him upend the bottle.

Listening to a minx who was whispering in her ear, Kelly climbed into Ben's lap and wrapped her legs around his waist. The fact that they still weren't wearing any clothes didn't bother her one bit. "So tell me something," she purred in his ear. "Isn't this much more enjoyable than sitting in some stuffy office?"

"We have an excellent air-conditioning

system," he pointed out, although thinking of anything so mundane as his office wasn't easy when a delectable naked woman was sitting in his lap, reawakening parts of him he thought were more than ready for a rest.

She wiggled for effect. "I bet your secretary doesn't sit in your lap for dictation."

"Barb would hit me if I suggested it." He nuzzled her throat, inhaling the warm, musky scent of her skin as it mingled with his own. He doubted that anything else in the world could be as wonderful as this, and his body seemed to agree wholeheartedly.

"I seem to be getting the impression that you aren't very tired," Kelly murmured, biting down on his earlobe.

Ben gripped her waist and raised her up, then down onto his waiting shaft. "It must be all those vegetables you fed me for dinner."

It was much later before Kelly could marvel over their luck that they hadn't been interrupted by anyone else desiring to picnic in such a private spot.

Still feeling brave, they ran into the water, splashing each other and rolling in the waves like two porpoises.

"You mean anyone could have just shown up here?" In spite of the warm night, Ben felt a frisson of cold travel down his spine.

Kelly laughed as she launched herself at him and draped her arms around his neck. "I told you, it's a favorite spot for those who know about it," she confided. "In fact, rumor has it that many babies have been conceived on this beach."

The thought of Kelly having his baby was scary and wonderful all at the same time. Luckily, Ben knew this wasn't the time to even consider the idea. He had to convince her of a few other things first.

"Come with me, Kelly. Come see my part of the world. Find out that I'm not all that bad when I'm in a business suit and dealing with my company." He sensed her withdrawal even before he saw her seem to pull within herself.

"You're acting pushy, Wyatt," she murmured, lifting her cup and swallowing her wine in one gulp.

"I'm asking." He wasn't about to hide the edge in his voice.

Kelly leaned forward and poured more wine into her cup. "Maybe I'll come visit you sometime."

"That's not what I asked and you damn well know it."

She looked up and easily read the anger that was coupled with frustration in his eyes. "If you want to see me, you know where I am."

She couldn't have chosen a more deliberate challenge. Ben pushed aside their picnic and moved closer to Kelly until his chest brushed against hers.

"Spit it out, Kelly," he ordered. "What exactly do you want from me? Are you happy making me crazy? Does it give you a thrill knowing that I'm always tied up in knots? That you taunt me until I wonder if I shouldn't just walk away before I throttle you? Why do you keep pushing me?"

"You act as if what I'm doing is some sort of deliberate provocation on my part."

He pulled his body away as if he couldn't stand to be close to her. "Maybe it is. Maybe you've got something against men and I'm the poor idiot chosen to suffer for someone else's sins." Muttering curses under his breath, he scrambled to his feet and walked down to the water. His shoulders heaved with his efforts to regain his temper as he stared out over the sea.

Kelly sat up and studied his back for several moments before getting to her feet. She walked toward him, stopping when she was within touching distance.

"I've never considered myself a vengeful person," she said softly, resisting the urge to touch him, to feel his muscles move under her hands. "No, I'm not punishing you for someone else's mistakes. That's not my style. I'm scared, Ben. I'm so afraid that if I leave this island my new identity and my new way of life will be taken from me. And I'm also afraid that if I see you in the setting you're used to, I'll see the man my father once was, and that will hurt just as much. When we're here, you're the laid-back personality it would be easy to fall in love with. There, you'll be the businessman dealing with meetings and all those day-to-day problems that go with the job, and pretty soon you'll be calling me, saying, "Sorry, babe, something's come up. I'll be a little late." Pretty soon, that 'little late' will turn even later. No, I won't be there to hear the excuses," she said without rancor. "I used to hear them a long time ago. That was enough."

He spun around so quickly she was taken off guard. "Is that what you think? You claim you're not punishing me, Kelly, but you are. You're punishing me because your father chose his work over you. I've always known what's important to me, and in just a very short time, you've proven to be *extremely* important to me. I just wish you'd believe it."

"I want to," she whispered, looking into his eyes.

"Then prove it and come to Sydney with me when I leave."

Kelly made no reply. She merely bent down and began picking up the mess that was scattered across the blanket.

"Well, I guess that's my answer then," Ben muttered, before bending down to help her.

Kelly should have been furious with Ben's demands, with his asking so much of her. So why was she still thinking about something that was basically over and done with?

The ride back to her house was quiet. Both of them were engrossed in their own thoughts: Kelly wondering if she really could leave the island after all the happiness and peace it had gifted her with, Ben fearing he had lost her after all.

He said nothing when he walked her to her

front door, but he did leave her with the kind of kiss that told her he hadn't given up hope.

Which was why Kelly was wandering about the darkened confines of her house at two o'clock in the morning. The peace of mind she'd always received from her surroundings was nowhere to be found. Hurricane Ben had swept into her life and created such a turmoil, she doubted she would ever be able to recapture it.

List the positives of going with him, Kelly.

Oh, that's easy. I'll be back in the big city with a faster-paced way of life, department stores within easy reach where I can quickly find anything I need, a large variety of restaurants, craft stores that carry all the things I normally have to mail-order months in advance. More than two hair salons to choose from. The chance to dress up once in a while and wear more than shorts and tank tops seven days a week. Need I go on?

Fine, and what if you stay here . . . without him.

Peace of mind, a more easygoing lifestyle that doesn't raise the blood pressure, the chance to hang on to my sanity.

Yes, but you'll be giving up some great sex. No matter what you say, sweetheart, the man is an incredible lover who really lights your fire. Are you sure you want to give that up? And, last but not least, you'll be lonely again.

In a fit of temper, Kelly picked up a ceramic ashtray and threw it on the floor, then watched it shatter into dozens of tiny pieces.

"If I wasn't going to smoke anymore, I shouldn't have kept you around," she informed the ruined receptacle before stooping down to pick up the pieces. For a moment, she remained in that uncomfortable position, staring down at the broken ashtray and thinking about the time she'd picked up the shattered pieces of her life. She'd gone on to make a new life for herself, hadn't she? Made a fresh start? So, why couldn't she do it again, in a new location? There wasn't any law that categorically stated she had to remain here.

"Maybe it's time to move on," she whispered.

TEN

"Compromising isn't easy for me."

Kelly was the last person Ben expected to find on the other side of the door. She stood there looking weary and bedraggled, still dressed in the rumpled clothing she'd worn on their evening picnic. What looked suspiciously like tearstains marred her cheeks and her color was pale instead of healthy. There was no sign of the self-confident woman he'd come to know so well.

He dragged his hand through his hair, creating some additional disarray of his own. He cleared his throat.

"It's not easy for anyone." He stepped back, gesturing for her to enter. He watched her walk in with slow, measured steps that suggested to him she'd come to a decision but still wasn't sure it was good for her.

Kelly walked over to the dining table and lightly ran her hand over the smooth polished surface.

"I've talked to you more about my inner self than I've talked to anyone else for a few years now," she murmured, still tracing odd patterns on the wood. "I always felt if someone knew my weak points they would use them against me."

He leaned back against the closed front door. "Aren't you afraid I'll do just that?"

"Not at all. That isn't your style."

Relief flooded his body as he heard her sincere reply. Her appearing on his doorstep in the middle of the night had given him hope; now her words gave him her answer, even if she hadn't said it out loud yet.

"Is that why you came over at three in the morning? To tell me you don't like to compromise and that I'm basically a nice guy?"

When she first looked up, her gaze was unfocused, as if she was still caught in another time frame. As her expression gradually cleared, she noticed that it *was* the middle of the night and that Ben clearly wasn't dressed for company. Unless the best-dressed businessmen were now wearing, zebra-striped jockey briefs. Her lips twitched.

"I like your pj's." She gestured toward him.

He shrugged. "I thought I should throw something on so I wouldn't shock whoever was pounding on the door. I guess I didn't need to worry."

"I'm pretty shockproof."

"I know."

Kelly curled a strand of stray hair around her fingertips. "If I don't like it you won't try to talk me out of coming back here?"

Ben slowly shook his head.

"You'll understand?"

"I'll do my best."

Kelly stared up at the ceiling as if she would find all her answers there. "You're so damned honest," she murmured. "You could have lied and said yes, but you had to speak the truth, didn't you?"

"You'd know if I lied to you."

"Yes, I would, wouldn't I?" She knew everything there was to know about him, not just what he told her, but what was inside him, because she could read him as easily as he could read her. "I really don't want to go back home this late."

Ben worked to keep his expression impassive. "You're welcome to stay here."

"I'd like to."

He straightened up and walked toward her with his hand outstretched. Kelly didn't hesitate in taking it as he led her down the small hallway to the master bedroom. The sheets were rumpled and the silk coverlet had been tossed on the floor, testimony of a restless sleep. Kelly unzipped her dress and let it drop before climbing into bed. Ben stretched out beside her and pulled the top sheet up to their waists before taking her in his arms and settling her head in the hollow of his shoulder. While he wanted nothing more than to make love to her again, he knew this was a time for her to rest. Besides, as far as he was concerned, they had a lifetime ahead of them. All he had to do was convince Kelly of that.

"You've turned my life upside down." Her words were slurred as weariness overtook her.

He brushed a kiss across her brow. "That goes both ways."

Kelly curved an arm around his waist as she settled in more comfortably and closed her eyes. "This is nice," she murmured just before she fell asleep.

He angled his face against the soft cloud of

her hair, silently ordering his body to behave. "Very nice."

The moment Kelly's senses came awake, she knew she wasn't in her bed. She didn't need the sound of a shower running nearby or the feel of silk sheets against her skin to tell her that. She opened one eye, then the other.

"This is incredible," she breathed, getting a good look at her surroundings.

"G'day. I see you're awake," Ben greeted her, walking out of the bathroom. A bright teal towel swathed his hips while he used another to dry his hair.

She pushed a stray lock of hair out of her face. "You can actually sleep here?"

Ben glanced around at the bright teal and purple wall hanging that decorated the wall opposite the bed. "Well, I admit it isn't easy, but I figured this way I'd never get drunk, because I knew I wouldn't be able to wake up with a hangover and see this without going insane. And the purple sheets are a bit much, too, aren't they?" He walked over to the table by the window. "Want some coffee?"

"Yes, thank you." His formal manner made her feel a bit uneasy.

Ben picked up the silver coffee server and poured the dark brew into a china cup. He didn't bother to pull open the drapes, instead leaving the room in a comfortable darkness. "Thank God the *china* isn't teal or purple." He smiled as he brought her the cup.

Kelly's smile turned puzzled as she reached for the cup, but Ben held it up, out of her reach.

"Kiss first, coffee next," he murmured, lowering his head.

"What about morning breath?"

"Don't worry, I already brushed my teeth." His mouth covered hers, his tongue demanding entrance as he nibbled and nipped her lips in his own idea of a morning feast. Without missing a beat, Ben placed the coffee cup on the nightstand and twisted his body to follow her back onto the sheets.

Kelly gripped his shoulder, pulling him even closer to her. "Good," she breathed, "because I think your idea is much better than coffee."

Ben traced a line across the tops of Kelly's breasts, following it with his mouth.

"And here I dragged myself out of bed and took a shower so I wouldn't give in to my baser instincts." He curled his tongue around one rosy nipple. "I should have followed my first one." He ran his hand across her abdomen.

Kelly moaned softly. She already knew that the slight calluses on the tips of his fingers lent an exciting roughness to his touch, but she could swear this time was different. She responded in kind by reacquainting herself with the crisp hair that covered his chest and arrowed downward. "Let's do away with this." She flicked the knot on his towel and slid it away. "Much better." She ran her fingernail along his waistline and downward to his steely length, which instantly responded to her touch.

Ben sucked in his breath at her intimate caress. "Yes," he hissed, rotating his hips in a motion that forecast things to come. "Love me back, Kelly."

"No problem."

He turned her blood to liquid fire as he began kissing every inch of her skin, murmuring appreciation for the faint freckles on her shoulders, whispering how silky her skin felt, praising her for her responsiveness as he found each aching spot, caressing her to ecstatic agony. He touched the fiery nub, sending sparks shooting through her veins, and he soothed that same fire with his tongue, which first cooled, then heated. He ignored Kelly's cries and whimpers.

"Soon," he promised in a dark whisper.

She pressed her open mouth against his shoulder. The tip of her tongue darted out, tasting the salt of his damp skin. "You're a devil."

"Convert me," he huskily invited. "Save me."

Kelly's laughter stuck in her throat. "But who will save me?"

Ben raised his hips, hovering at the entrance of what he privately considered paradise. "I guess we'll just have to save each other." He entered her slowly. He wanted to savor the liquid heat surrounding him, but he couldn't. Not when her body pulled him inward so easily, so irresistibly.

Kelly wrapped her arms and legs around him, refusing to let him go and refusing to allow him to take it slow and easy. Each thrust sent them deeper into the flames until neither knew where one began and the other stopped.

Ben's chest heaved with badly needed air as he rolled to one side, after first making sure Kelly was nestled against him. He massaged her nape with his fingertips, kneaded the damp hair.

"Hey." Kelly rubbed her cheek against his chest.

He closed his eyes in an effort to keep the magic they'd just shared within his soul. "How can you even think of talking after what we just had?"

"I'm not," she murmured, running her palm across his abdomen. His muscles tightened in reaction. "It's just that you promised me I could have my coffee after you kissed me."

"Coffee? You want coffee?" he growled, rolling over and playfully digging his fingers into her waist. Kelly howled with laughter and tried to squirm out of his hold. "Oh, so the lady is ticklish! Are you ticklish all over?"

"No!" she shrieked. "Stop it, Ben!"

"Not until I find out just where you aren't ticklish." He attacked another sensitive spot, easily evading her punishing fists and her orders to stop.

By the time Ben discovered there weren't any spots that weren't ticklish, Kelly's coffee was stone cold and it was past time for lunch.

"I look ridiculous," Kelly muttered, looking down at the baggy shorts and T-shirt she was wearing.

"You look cute," Ben corrected, proving his point with a kiss on her nose.

"I would have been better off wearing my dress, wrinkles and all, instead of your clothes." She plucked the shirt away from her chest. "I guess I shouldn't feel that self-conscious. It's not as if I'm sneaking out of here wearing an evening gown." She straightened up when the elevator doors slid open.

"Just act as if you're wearing the height of resort wear," Ben whispered in her ear.

He halted their procession across the lobby long enough to check in at the shop space to see if the painting was coming along, then walked her outside.

"I'd like to drive you home," he told her, keeping his arms loosely looped around her waist.

She shook her head. "I can easily ride my bike back. Besides, you know you need to stay here and interview applicants to run the shop. And I need to get back to my own work."

Ben wanted to reassure himself that she wouldn't forget her promise to come to Sydney with him, but he knew that would only force her to think he doubted her.

"Dinner tonight?"

She grimaced. "It's my night at the Rusty Nail. I try to get down there a few nights a week. You're welcome to come down—as long as you promise to stay out of trouble." She poked him in the chest with her forefinger to punctuate her warning.

He grabbed her hand and lifted the punishing finger to his lips. "I'll do my best, as long as you give me one of those special smiles of yours."

She happily complied. "I seem to be doing a lot of that today."

This time he dropped his kiss on her lips, not her nose, but it was by no means light or carefree. This kiss involved a bit of nipping and more than a little heavy breathing, on both their parts.

"I better let you go before I think about dragging you back into the hotel," he rasped, stepping back. "As it is, I didn't even feed you breakfast."

"Yes you did. It turned very cold, though, while we were in the shower. As for dragging me back, that might not be such a good idea, since the maid was entering your suite while we were waiting for the elevator," she reminded him. "But come by the Rusty Nail and I'll buy you a drink."

"Don't worry, I'll be there—if only to protect you from drunken customers."

Kelly rolled her eyes at that. "Trust me, Del does that very well." She turned around and walked toward a bicycle leaning against a palm tree.

Ben couldn't help it. He had to stay there and watch her ride down the road until he could no longer see her. Thoughts of his family popped into his head. He'd received more than a few calls lately asking when he'd be coming home.

"Surprise, Mom, I'm bringing home a lady," he murmured, before turning around and walking back into the hotel.

Kelly walked into the Rusty Nail earlier than usual and found only a few customers, knowing it wouldn't begin to fill up until early evening. Del stood at the bar talking to one of the fishermen. When he saw his boss he nodded a greeting and went back to his conversation.

Kelly retrieved the ledgers from behind the bar, poured herself a diet cola, and walked over to the table she considered hers, where she spread out the ledgers and invoices.

"Here a bit early, aren't you, boss?" Del said, taking the chair across from her.

"I wanted to talk to you before it got too busy," she said.

"Yeah, that was one thing I was going to talk to you about. It's been gettin' so busy some nights I really could use a second guy behind the bar. Ray said his brother's been looking for a job up at the resort, but his looks've been puttin' people off."

"I can imagine so," Kelly said dryly. "What was it? The cobra tattoo on his right arm, the naked-woman tattoo on his left arm, the obviously-broken-too-many-times nose, or his missing front teeth?"

Del shrugged. "Who knows? But what I *do* know is he's honest and can swing a mean left hook when things get rough."

"I'd say it's up to you."

He looked puzzled. "But you're the boss. You should make the decision."

"Yes, you're right, the boss should make the decision." Kelly reached into her purse and pulled out a folded sheet of paper, handing it to him. "If you like what's written there, you're more than welcome to make that decision about Ray's brother."

Del unfolded the sheet of paper and began

reading the typed words. He looked stunned as it dawned on him what they meant.

"You want to sell me the bar?"

"Only if you want it," she replied. "When you began working for me you told me you were only going to stay long enough to save up enough money to buy one of your own. This will just speed up the process."

Del shook his head, still trying to take it all in. "I don't have near enough money to pay what it's worth," he ruefully admitted. "And we both know I'd never get a loan for what I'd need."

"That's why I'm suggesting you pay me out of your profits," she said, pointing to a particular paragraph. "Business has really picked up the past few months, so there shouldn't be any problem in your meeting the payment schedule."

"But why do you want to sell the bar? You always claimed you got a big kick out of ownin' it." He dropped the paper onto the table. "No, I can't do it."

"I've decided to make some changes in my life, Del," she said quietly. "One of them is getting rid of the Rusty Nail, because I don't think I'll be here much longer."

Del's beefy face showed alarm. "What's wrong? Are you sick or somethin'?"

Kelly bit her lip to keep from laughing. If he only knew that she'd once thought she was very sick. "No, but I'll be leaving the island." She picked the paper up and handed it to him. "If you're agreeable to the terms, we can have this typed up in legalese and made official."

"Why would you want to leave?" Del asked, ignoring her words. "You said you never wanted to go back to the States. That this place gave you life again."

"It did," she admitted. "But I've been doing a lot of thinking lately, and I've come to realize it's time to move on."

"It's that Aussie, isn't it? He's the reason you want to leave. Are you going with him?"

Kelly wasn't offended by his blunt questions. She knew he only asked out of regard for her. "Yes."

"Are you going to marry him?"

"We haven't gotten that far yet. Besides, you know how I feel about marriage."

Del's face widened in a broad grin. "That night we got snockered and confessed our life stories," he chuckled. "You about your marriage to that actor. Me about my years bouncing in and out of prison. I'm surprised you didn't fire me that night."

"No reason to. You're a good bartender,

you don't drink on the job, and you don't
make passes at the female customers. So, are
you interested?"

"I'd be stupid not to be." He stuck out his
hand. "You've got a deal."

As Kelly shook his hand, she felt the ties
holding the island breaking, one strand at a
time.

"So Del's going to be one of the new entre-
preneurs of the island." Looking like a happy pasha as he stretched out on the chaise
longue, Ben accepted the glass of wine Kelly
handed him.

"He'll make it. I know he will." She nudged
his hip with her knee. "Move over." When he
obliged, she slid alongside him, plucked his
glass out of his hand, and sipped the wine.

"You couldn't get one of your own?"

"No—sharing is much more intimate." Her
voice lowered to a husky purr on the last word.
She stuck her forefinger in the glass and painted
Ben's lower lip with the wine, then leaned over
and delicately licked it off.

His eyes turned a dark jade. "Your selling
the bar makes me think you don't intend to
come back here. I didn't mean for you to break

all the ties you've made on Treasure Cove. I don't want you to blame me for leaving."

"I know that," she said simply. "I just feel it's time to make some changes in my life and that leaving the island is necessary to do that. I've used my time here to heal, and now it's time to move on into another phase of my life. Here, take this back." She handed him his wine and methodically began to work each button of his shirt loose and to spread it open. Where her hands led, her lips quickly followed, blazing a trail over the hair-roughened skin, seeking out a flat copper nipple that soon rose up under her gentle nibbles.

"Kelly." He tried to move to put the glass down before it spilled.

"Just relax, enjoy, and drink your wine," she murmured, tracing the zipper tab before slowly lowering it.

Pretty soon, Ben could have cared less if he drank the wine, if it spilled, or if it just disappeared into thin air.

ELEVEN

"I'm very impressed," Kelly complimented Ben as she walked through the shop's interior. Instead of empty space, racks of clothing lined the walls, interspersed with accessories designed to tempt the buyer to buy one or more of them to spice up her new outfit. "I can't believe it's the same place."

"Amazing what a little paint and wallpaper can do." Ben was pleased by her show of pleasure.

"No, it's much more than that and you know it." She arched an eyebrow at the elaborate display of her hand-painted clothing set up in a prominent corner.

He held up his hands, palms out to show innocence. "Your work is popular."

Kelly looked around at the soft blue and green swirls on the walls that made one feel they were in the middle of a lagoon. It was soft and soothing to the senses and offset the bold, colorful clothing at the same time.

"No wonder you do so well with your shops: They fairly drag you in to browse, and ultimately buy."

He followed her example of modesty. "I'd forgotten how much work—work that can also be fun—setting up a store can be," he murmured. "With my first three stores, I did it all, from finding and leasing space to overseeing all the decorating. As the company grew, I had to start delegating work to others and concentrating on the administrative end." He walked over to some glass cases containing a variety of costume jewelry.

"Then you'll just have to 'do it all' again the next time you open a new boutique," Kelly suggested.

He shook his head. "No, I think this will be the last one. I'd rather concentrate on keeping all of them up-to-date."

She licked her lips, silently blaming their dryness on the air-conditioning. "All that's left is the grand opening tomorrow."

"That's right."

"When do you want to go to Sydney?"

"I need to get back to my office by the first of next week." He studied her from across the room, watching her as if trying to gauge her mood.

Three days. She thought of how much she had to do in three days. She suddenly wondered if she was doing the right thing. Then she looked up and saw Ben, with those wonderful craggy features, those deep emerald eyes that always seemed to sparkle with lights, that smile that always turned her bones to jelly.

"I wonder how I'll manage in a big city again."

It wasn't until she saw his body visibly relax that she realized he'd been tense, as if fearing the worst.

"Remember, it's only a trial run," she thought to warn him.

"You can come to my office and watch me tell the others what to do," he offered. "I'm wonderful at delegating work."

"For the past three weeks I've watched you throw your all into getting the boutique ready in time," she reminded him. "Some nights you've gone to bed so exhausted you couldn't sleep. You spent three hours on the phone one day because a shipment was misplaced. It seemed to me you were falling back into old habits."

His jaw tightened. "Those were problems only I could solve, and you know it."

Kelly stood in front of him and pressed her palm against his cheek. "I guess I'll just have to provide you with a good reason to leave your office in the evening, won't I?" She inhaled the slight spicy scent of his skin.

He pulled her into his arms. "I don't think you'll have any problem on that count, since I'll be leaving it to come home to you."

Her first reaction to the big city was an aversion to all the noise that assaulted ears unused to so much activity. Car engines revving, horns honking, everyone talking. And all the buildings that hovered over her. She had never felt so relieved as when they entered the quiet haven of Ben's house.

"What do you think?" He was busy paying the taxi driver, who had deposited their luggage in the entryway.

"I had no idea how much I had cut myself off from the world until now," she murmured, walking across the living room to the floor-to-ceiling windows that overlooked the bay.

"Do you feel like you're suffering from overload?" Ben walked up behind her and wrapped his arms around her waist, pulling her back toward him.

She closed her eyes, savoring his closeness. "Something like that. I can't believe I never used to notice any of it. The noise, the auto pollution, just everything to do with a big city. I feel so out of place, out of step with the times." Her breasts rose and fell with a huge sigh. "I'm whining, aren't I?"

Ben chuckled. "No. Between getting up early so we wouldn't miss our connecting flight and being on the run since then—not to mention the time change—it's no wonder you feel out of sorts."

"That's it, I'm just tired," she grumbled, punching his clasped hands without any heat in her motion.

"Why don't you have a nice hot bath and rest up before you see the rest of the house?"

"Aah. I feel better already."

"All the bedrooms have adjoining baths."

She leaned her head back against his chest. "Which bedroom has the most comfortable bed?"

"The master bedroom, naturally."

"Is it one of the rooms mentioned?"

"I wanted you to make the choice," he said quietly.

"I just hope you're neater here than you were at my house."

"I'm not that bad."

She turned around in the loose circle of his arms. "Oh, no? Then why did I used to find wet towels all over the bathroom and dirty socks hanging on the lamp shades."

"I never hung my dirty socks on the lamp shade," he defended himself in a huffy tone.

"Only because you probably didn't think of it and you rarely wore socks." She smiled. "Thank you. I feel more like myself now."

"Come on, I'll show you to the bedroom and you can relax in the tub while I get us some wine." He released her and gathered up her luggage. "Are you sure you brought enough? I'd hate to have you run out of clothes too soon."

Kelly laughed at his expression as he gazed at the small duffel bag and tote she had brought along. "I plan to do a lot of shopping after I check in with Elaine," she explained.

"Then it's probably a good thing the phone has an extra-long cord, so you can talk from the tub if you want to." He led the way down a hallway to the room at the end. Double doors opened into a room that appeared to be equal to the size of his hotel suite.

"Very impressive, Wyatt." Kelly circled the room, peeked in the walk-in closets, glanced into the bathroom, and slid open glass doors to walk out onto the balcony. She turned around and leaned back with her hands curled around the railing. "All right, give me time to relax and clean up while you call your office."

"I hadn't planned on calling my office, since I'll be going in tomorrow morning."

"And if they need you for something today?"

"They won't. They're all so capable of handling anything that comes along, I sometimes joke I feel like a figurehead there," he told her.

She shook her head, looking all too knowing. "Don't kid a kidder. You've probably been away from your office longer than you ever have before. Naturally you're going to want to check in and make sure it's still there." She pushed herself away from the railing and reentered the room. "Go ahead, I understand."

Ben dropped her duffel bag on the bed. "Feel free to use the closet on the left," was all he said before walking out.

Kelly knew he was angry with her, but she'd had to say it. Ben hadn't said a word about getting in touch with his office, but she couldn't imagine he wouldn't want to call in and find out what was going on.

"Men can be so confusing," she sighed, unzipping her bag and pulling out a robe and a container of bath salts. Bath first, then a call to Elaine to tell her her whereabouts so she wouldn't worry if she couldn't get ahold of Kelly. Wasn't she going to be in for a surprise to find out Kelly had finally left the island!

"If I'd had my way I wouldn't have come out of that bathroom for the next two days," Kelly announced a little over an hour later as she walked into the family room, where Ben sat relaxing on the couch while listening to the stereo.

"I've always thought it's a bit too much. Would you like something to drink?"

"Anything cold and nonalcoholic." She dropped into a nearby easy chair, settling the folds of her robe around her legs. "Now, this room is more like you."

He looked pleased at her insight. "I didn't allow the decorator to do anything in here. I wanted a room I could hide in. The rest is for show." He handed her an ice-filled glass.

She smiled as she accepted the glass of diet cola. "At least you didn't end up with strobe lights."

He smiled at the shared joke. "Did your bath revive you?"

"I feel more like myself." A suspicious thought crept into her mind. "Why?"

"My mom called and wants us to come over for dinner."

Her eyes grew huge. "Tonight?"

" 'Fraid so. Don't worry, she doesn't bite. She thought a family evening would be a good chance for you to get to know everyone before the party."

She sat forward. "What party?"

"The one she wants to give for us."

"Ben." Her tone warned him of future punishment if he didn't explain.

"I'm not known for going off on business trips and bringing back women. She just wants to get to know you. Don't worry, my mother isn't one of those society dowagers. Her blood is your run-of-the-mill red and she likes nothing more than cooking for a crowd. She'll probably tell you you're too thin and insist you have a second helping of dessert."

Kelly curled her arms around his neck and pulled him down into the chair with her. "A second helping of dessert, huh? The things I'll do for you."

"Kelly, I feel as if I already know you! Your work is so lovely." Sarah Wyatt gave Kelly the same enthusiastic hug she'd given her son. "My dear, you are so thin," she clucked. "I know it's popular with you girls nowadays, but I never considered it healthy." She took Kelly by the arm and led her through the house.

The older woman had Ben's green eyes and her own brown hair, now heavily streaked with gray. His father greeted Kelly with Ben's smile, and she could look at him and see Ben in thirty-odd years.

She easily relaxed as Sarah peppered her with questions about her fabric painting and about Los Angeles while refusing any help from Kelly and putting the finishing touches on dinner.

"We flew out there about a year ago, taking the grandchildren as a special treat for them—and for their parents, who had time to themselves for three weeks." She spoke of the eighteen-hour flight as if it had been a short hop. "We took the children to all the sights, from Disneyland to Universal Studios to Sea

World. That was more than enough for me in my lifetime!" she said as she dished out a hearty beef stew and dumplings.

"It can be a bit overpowering," Kelly admitted, feeling a bit overpowered by the chattering woman.

Sarah didn't stop talking once during dinner, dispensing bits of Ben's childhood—some of which he loudly complained were embarrassing—and asking Kelly more questions about herself.

"I am so glad you dumped that Michael," she said bluntly.

"Mom!" Ben looked ready to explode.

"I am," she said to her son, then turned back to Kelly, who looked as if she'd fallen down a rabbit hole and ended up in Wonderland. "We get a few of your soap operas over here, although I gather we receive them a bit later in the year than you do. Personally, I don't think he can act. All he can do is walk around with his shirt off and smile at the women. Why, he looked like a wooden Indian when he was in bed with that Lotta."

Kelly bit her lower lip, but it was useless. Laughter spilled out, full and rich. "No, she's right." She placed her hand on Ben's arm as he leaned forward to reprimand his mother. "Michael can't act his way out of a paper bag. The way I hear it, he's about to receive a very nasty disfiguring disease," she confided.

The older woman's eyes lit up at the idea of hearing a wonderful secret. "Really?"

Kelly nodded. "The viewers have been asking for more, and he just isn't giving it to them. I'm sure the writers will give him a wonderful funeral."

Sarah looked at her son. "Ben, you've rarely brought your ladies home to meet us, but I'm sure glad you brought this one over." She looked from one to the other with open speculation in her eyes.

"Enough, Sarah," Josh, Ben's father, inserted. "You're embarrassing the poor girl and probably making Ben wish they'd stayed home tonight."

"I can't believe those were practically the only words your father said all evening," Kelly told Ben later as they drove back to his house.

"Dad doesn't say a whole lot, probably because Mom *does*, but when he does talk, she always stops and listens." Affection warmed his voice. "They're great."

"Yes, I can see that." Kelly vainly tried to cover her mouth as she yawned widely.

His hand reached out in the darkness to wrap itself around her neck and knead the tired muscles. "You've had a long day."

She nodded, but even that seemed to take too much effort. "I'm sure somewhere in this crazy world, it's past my bedtime."

He nudged her head down to his shoulder. "Then close your eyes."

Kelly had barely closed her eyes before she fell into so deep a sleep that she didn't awaken when Ben picked her up out of the car and carried her into the house. Nor did she stir when he stripped off her clothing, dropped one of his T-shirts over her, and later stretched out next to her. A murmur left her lips when he pulled her into his arms.

"Good night, love." He brushed a kiss against her brow.

"Mmm." She smiled and snuggled in closer.

"Now that I've got you here, I'm not letting you go!" he vowed softly, keeping her in a warm embrace.

"Are you listening to me?"

Ben looked up. "Of course I am, Barb," he

said to the woman who stood on the other side of his desk.

"Then repeat back to me what I told you."

He opened his mouth, then closed it. "I don't like smart-aleck secretaries."

"Personal assistant," she corrected. "A personal assistant who richly deserves a raise for putting up with a boss who's only here physically, meaning *I* have to pick up the slack!"

"Fine, you've got a raise."

Barb leaned across the desk and placed her palm across his forehead. "Just checking to see if you have a fever. Since you don't, I'm going out to type up the paperwork for my raise."

Ben looked up just as Barb disappeared out of sight. "Raise? What raise?"

Barb appeared in the doorway. "Boss, you've been back for almost a week and you haven't accomplished a day's worth of work. I just want you to know that your being in love is making the rest of us crazy. Today's the worst so far, and it's barely nine o'clock!"

He grinned. "That bad, huh?"

"Worse. Get things settled with the lady so things can return to normal around here, okay?" she ordered. "Now I'm going to type up my salary-raise paperwork!"

"I never said you could have a raise!"

"Yes you did."

"Never get any respect," he grumbled, staring with unseeing eyes at the stack of paperwork in front of him. Sighing, he forced himself to concentrate on his work, which wasn't easy when it was competing with pictures of Kelly naked in his bed that morning and of what went on before he finally dragged himself off to the office.

"Why should you—you're only the boss!" Barb quipped from the outer office just as the phone rang. She chirped merrily into the receiver. "Randy wants to know if you're 'in' to Ms. Andrews," she said, referring to the building's security guard.

"Very funny," he growled, straightening up.

"Hi, Barb." He heard Kelly's husky voice before he saw her. "How is he today?"

"Making all of us crazy, so please take him away."

Ben jumped up from his chair and ran into the outer office. "I heard that." He passed his accusing gaze over both women.

"If you can get away I'll treat you to lunch," Kelly suggested.

"I'm already gone." Ben took her arm and led her to the bank of elevators.

Barb answered the phone, covered the receiver, and called Ben's name. "It's Mr. Herman about that shipment of bathing suits."

"Ryan should be handling that. Tell him you'll transfer him to Ryan's office," Ben called back before stepping into the waiting elevator.

"You weren't kidding when you said you believe in delegating." Kelly had waited until they were seated at the restaurant before bringing the subject up. "You could have taken the call, you know. I do understand that some things in business can't wait."

Ben shook his head. "I don't handle that end, and haven't in a long time. Trouble is, Rob Herman figures because he's one of our largest suppliers he should receive preferential treatment. I have staff to deal with different parts of the business. They're much happier when I don't interfere with their departments." He cocked his head to one side. "So why don't you tell me how much you've missed me today."

Kelly dug into her spinach salad with hot bacon dressing instead. "I've been too busy spending lots of money and seeing the city." One running argument they'd been having was that Kelly refused to let Ben show her the city, insisting that she preferred doing it on her own or with his mother, whom she already considered a good friend. She twirled her fork among the green leaves. "The shelves were delivered and set up today."

"How does the room look now?"

"Just the way you hoped: the kind of studio any artist would love to have."

He thought of the diamond ring he had so carefully selected for her. The one he'd been burning to give her for days now while he waited for the right time. He decided his waiting was over. "Do you love it enough to stay?"

She carefully set her fork down, then blotted her lips before speaking. "You live in a beautiful city, have very nice friends, own a business that's obviously growing yet doesn't consume you, and it's become difficult to remember a time when you weren't in my life," she said quietly.

"And you love me."

She smiled and shook her head. "Your arrogance is so astounding."

"Not where you're concerned," he said without arrogance, sounding instead like a man afraid of losing something that had grown very precious to him. "I thought we'd have dinner out this evening, if that's all right with you."

"It sounds wonderful."

❧ ———————— ❧

Kelly dressed early so she would be ready when Ben got home. While she waited for him, she wandered through the large room that Ben had set up for her studio. Floor-to-ceiling windows on three sides, a huge skylight, a large worktable, a stereo system along the fourth wall . . . She touched each piece before moving to one of the windows, where, engrossed in her thoughts, she didn't hear Ben calling her name.

"Do you enjoy standing in the dark?" He reached over and flipped the light switch.

She turned around when the overhead light came on. The stunned look on Ben's face told her her choice of a dress had been perfect.

"You look fantastic," he breathed, walking toward her. He grasped her hands and held her arms out. "I'm almost afraid to touch you."

"Touching's the best part."

He cleared his throat. "I better change my clothes fast before I change my mind about our going out."

Later, Ben did not remember showering or dressing. All he remembered was wanting to get back to the shimmering gold vision that was Kelly.

When they entered the restaurant, every

man turned to look at her. And who could blame them? Ben thought. Kelly was easily the most beautiful woman there.

"It seems your shopping was a success," he commented once they were seated.

"Yes, it was."

Kelly's slip of a dress was a stretch gold Lurex that skimmed her slender curves, topped by a gold lace blazer. The gold theme was picked up again by her shimmery hose and high-heeled sandals. One side of her hair was pulled back, a gold comb holding the curls in place. The perfume she wore was heavier, more sophisticated, than her usual scent, and obviously meant to drive Ben crazy.

"I felt I should wear something special," she murmured.

His nerves seemed to pop out of his skin. Did she feel it too?

The idea of how the evening would end hovered over them, injecting them with a delicious sense of anticipation. They ate, they toasted each other, and they danced, but dinner now seemed just a prelude.

"Life here is hectic, but in a way, not as hectic as L.A.," Kelly told him as they opted for a walk before going back into the house. "Funny, I was so afraid that once I got back to the big city I'd feel the need to rush back into my old ways, but I don't feel it. I still enjoy sleeping late, and have no desire to start smoking again or to visit a broker's office. I wandered through the city and came up with some new ideas for my artwork, and then I walked into your office and realized that while you work very hard, you aren't driven. You do something I wasn't able to in the business world—divide work and play." She rested her head against his shoulder while feeling his hand warmly gripping hers.

Ben stopped short and spun her into his arms. "Does this mean what I think it means?"

She chuckled. "If you think I'm going to give up that gorgeous studio after all the work we've both put into it, you are very wrong. Ben!" she squealed. "You're going to break my ribs!"

"Yes!" he shouted, spinning her around in a dizzying circle. "Kelly, you said exactly what I wanted to hear." He stopped and lowered his mouth to hers.

Kelly's lips parted under his insistent touch. They clung to each other, hands running over each other's body.

"This is crazy!" Ben said, finally pulling his lips away. "The house is right over there."

Kelly slipped off her shoes and ran with Ben back to the house. Practically tearing each other's clothing off, they made their way to the bedroom.

Kelly looked up at Ben as he loomed over her.

"I love you."

She didn't stop saying the words the entire time his body thrust into hers, said them even louder every time she arched upward to meet him with equal force. Their bodies were soaked with perspiration by the time they parted.

"You'll have to marry me." Ben wasn't about to take no for an answer. He suddenly laughed. "I meant to propose to you over dinner and give you your ring. It's in my pants pocket."

"I think your pants are still in the living room." She rolled over and leaned her knee against his legs. "And yes, you horrible, arrogant man, I will marry you, but for one reason only." She raised up enough to pepper his face with kisses.

He flashed her his cocky grin. "That's easy. Because you love me."

"No, because you need someone who's

strong enough to knock that arrogance down every so often," she informed him, running her hand down his damp chest and below to caress him in a way that told him a second go-round wasn't all that far off. He knew it wouldn't be difficult, since he only had to look at her, to inhale that womanly fragrance of hers, to feel aroused.

Ben could only laugh. "Well, then, I guess our marriage won't be boring." He lifted his head and nipped her earlobe. "Maybe you'll give me a break on your work now. You know, family discount?"

Kelly's eyes gleamed a molten gold. "No way, buster." As she continued caressing him and dotting kisses along his jawline, she murmured, "I'm afraid we do have one problem."

By then Ben could have cared less what it was. "I can't see any problems."

"Oh, no, not with us," she breathed in his ear. "Actually, it has something to do with these two lawsuits pending against me. . . ."

THE EDITOR'S CORNER

Dear Readers,

If you loved our **BAD BOYS** last year, wait till you get a taste of our November LOVESWEPTs: **DANGEROUS MEN!** From a mysterious undercover state trooper to a roguish football player and a wilder-than-wild oil field wildcatter, these men thrive on danger, live on the edge, and push passion right past the limit! Like our heroines, you'll find it impossible to resist the sheer thrill of a walk on the wild side with men who are definitely *not* what your mother had in mind! With bold seduction and promises of passion, November's six heroes will sweep our heroines—and you—off your feet and into the fantasy of being loved by a Dangerous Man. . . .

Leanne Banks has created our first Dangerous Man in the sultry tale she calls **DANCE WITH THE DEVIL,** LOVESWEPT #648. Garth Pendleton was a

ILLEGAL MOTION, LOVESWEPT #651, is as good as they come. Football star Nick Logan was desperate enough to try anything to clear his name, and he figured he could intimidate or charm the truth out of Willa Trask—until he was burned by the sparks that flared between him and the beautiful redhead! He'd hired her to rehabilitate his injured knee, vowing to discover if she'd helped frame him—but instead of an ice princess, he found in her a wanton witch who touched his soul. When you've read this winning story, I'm sure you'll become big fans of Donna Kauffman!

We turn from a rookie to an all-star pro for our next Dangerous Man. Let the heartbreaking emotion of Laura Taylor sweep you away with **WILDER'S WOMAN**, LOVESWEPT #652. Craig Wilder—uncivilized, untamed, he'd paid a high price for survival. He'd meant to teach Chelsea Lockridge a lesson, to punish his ex-wife for her betrayal, but he hadn't anticipated the erotic torment of molding his body to hers—nor imagined the tenderness still buried deep inside his battered heart! She'd braved the wilderness and a storm with evidence that could deliver the justice Craig had been denied, but Chelsea wanted to prove she'd never lost faith in him . . . or her reckless passion for the man who could make her purr with pleasure. Branded for all eternity by a lover whose scars ran deep, she vowed she could help Craig mourn the past and trust her again by fighting his demons with the sweet fury of her love. Laura's deeply moving tale will capture you, heart and soul.

If you like your men *truly* dangerous, Glenna McReynolds has the mystery man for you in **AVENGING ANGEL**, LOVESWEPT #653. Bruised and bloody, Dylan Jones has driven a thousand miles with her name on his lips, desperate to save Johanna Lane from being murdered! The secrets she knew made her bad boy who was definitely out of Erin Lindsey's league. Everything about him was a dare and Erin trembled at the danger of caring for a man whose darkest secret was tangled with her own shadowed past. Garth felt he'd waited for Erin forever and wanted to give her back her lost dreams, but if she knew the pain that haunted him, he feared the woman who'd slipped inside his lonely heart might slip away. This tempting tale is sure to please all of you who helped to make Leanne's January 1993 LOVESWEPT a #1 bestseller.

Doris Parmett's electrifying heroes and heroines have never been so highly-charged as they are in **BAD ATTITUDE**, LOVESWEPT #649. Reid Cameron was a heartbreaker cop who kissed like the hero of a hot romance. He'd invaded Polly Sweet's privacy—and her fantasies—when he'd commandeered her house to catch a jewel thief, but when he decided they'd play lovers and then tried to teach the feisty spitfire a lesson about feigning passion, both were shocked by the fireworks their lips set off! Doris is in top form with this sizzling story.

Longtime favorite author Patt Bucheister will tempt and tease you to distraction with her **TAME A WILDCAT**, LOVESWEPT #650. Ryder Knight had always thrived on the adventure of being a wildcatter, relished the pursuit of a new oil well, but he felt his restlessness vanish when Hannah Corbett told him he looked like trouble—and that he was no gentleman! But when his possessive embrace made her go up in flames, she feared losing control, trading her freedom for the joy only he could teach her. Patt will keep you on the edge of your seat for every page of this one!

We at LOVESWEPT are always pleased to welcome a talented new writer to our pages, and we're sure you'll agree that Donna Kauffman, author of a target, and he was her best chance of getting out alive—even if it meant abducting the lady and keeping her with him against her will. Frightened and furious, Johanna was stunned to realize she knew her captor . . . and once had even desired him! Dylan gambled his life to feel her heat and taste the forbidden fruit of her lips and Johanna longed to repay the debt. I can't think of a better way to end your month of **DANGEROUS MEN** than with Glenna's **AVENGING ANGEL**!

So hang on to your hearts—next month six **DANGEROUS MEN** are coming to steal them away!

Happy reading,

Nita Taublib

Nita Taublib

Associate Publisher

P.S. Don't miss the exciting women's fiction Bantam has coming in November—sensual seduction in Susan Johnson's **OUTLAW;** love and black magic over the centuries in **MOONLIGHT, MADNESS, AND MAGIC** by LOVESWEPT authors Suzanne Forster, Charlotte Hughes, and Olivia Rupprecht; and a classic Fayrene Preston romance, **SATIN AND STEELE.** We'll be giving you a sneak peek at these terrific books in next month's LOVESWEPTs. And immediately following this page, look for a preview of the spectacular women's fiction books from Bantam *available now!*

Don't miss these exciting books by your favorite Bantam authors

On sale in September:
A WHISPER OF ROSES
by *Teresa Medeiros*

TENDER BETRAYAL
by *Rosanne Bittner*

THE PAINTED LADY
by *Lucia Grahame*

OREGON BROWN
by *Sara Orwig*

And in hardcover from Doubleday
SEIZED BY LOVE
by *Susan Johnson*

Teresa Medeiros

nationally bestselling author of
ONCE AN ANGEL
and HEATHER AND VELVET

presents

A WHISPER OF ROSES

"From humor to adventure, poignancy to passion, tenderness to sensuality, Teresa Medeiros writes rare love stories to cherish."—*Romantic Times*

Set in the wild Highlands of Scotland, this captivating historical romance is bursting with the breathtaking passion, sparkling humor, and enchanting atmosphere that have made Teresa Medeiros a bestselling author. It tells the heartbreaking tale of two lovers torn between their passion and the clan rivalry that divides their families.

The door behind him crashed open into the opposite wall, and Morgan swung around to find himself facing yet another exotic creature of myth.

A princess, her cloud of dark hair tumbled loose around her shoulders, the light behind her throwing every curve beneath her ivory nightdress into magnificent relief. Her delicate fingers were curled not around a scepter, but around the engraved hilt of a ceremonial claymore.

Silvery fingers of moonlight caressed the five feet of steel that lay between her hands and his heart.

"Hold your ground, rogue MacDonnell," she sweetly snarled. "One careless step and I'll be forced to take your head downstairs without the rest of you."

Morgan didn't even feel the pain as the crystal rose

snapped in his clumsy hands, embedding its stem deep in his palm.

"Why, you clumsy oaf! Look what you've gone and done now!"

Morgan's gaze automatically dropped to his hands. A jagged shard of glass protruded from his palm. Warm blood trickled down his wrist and forearm to puddle on one of Elizabeth Cameron's precious rugs. Before he could quench it, the old shame flared. Shame for being a MacDonnell. Shame for being such a crude ox. Just as quickly on its heels followed rage—the crushing rage that shielded his tattered pride from every blow. But before he could unleash it on the hapless girl, she dropped the sword and rushed over to him.

Tossing the splintered remains of the rose aside without a second glance, she cradled his hand in hers and dabbed at the wound with a wad of her nightdress. Her little hand was warm and soft and silky smooth beneath his own. "You really should take more care," she chided. "If you'd have struck your wrist, you might have bled to death."

Morgan was too dumbfounded by her concern to point out her illogic. If she'd have cut off his head, he might have bled to death even quicker. Still scowling over his hand, she dragged him toward the pale circle of light at the window.

"Be very still," she commanded. "I'm going to try to fish out this piece of glass. It's bound to be painful. You may scream if you like. I shan't think any less of you."

Since she'd never thought much of him to begin with, Morgan wasn't concerned. He didn't even flinch when she pressed his palm with her thumb and snagged the sliver of glass between the polished crescents of her fingernails.

Thoroughly bemused, Morgan studied her in the moonlight. The top of her head barely came to his chest. The spiral curls he used to yank with such relish tumbled down her back in inky waves. Her skin was fair except for the faintest hint of color, as if God had brushed rose petals across her cheeks and lips. A fringe of ebony silk shuttered her eyes. Her scent filled his nostrils, and he was shocked to feel his throat tighten with a primal hunger. She smelled like her mother, but fresher, sweeter. Some primitive male instinct warned him this was a bloom still on the vine, fragrant and tender and ripe. He frowned. She might be nectar to another man, but to him, Dougal Cameron's daughter would be as deadly as nightshade.

Her teeth cut into her lower lip as if to bite back a cry of her own as she drew forth the shard of glass and stanched the bleeding with yet another wad of her nightdress. Morgan feared he might soon have more of it twined around his arm than she had around her body. But an intriguing glimpse of a slender calf silenced his protest.

Grimacing, she lay the bloody splinter on the window-sill before glancing up at him.

At that moment, he cocked his head to the side, giving her an unobstructed view of his face. Moonlight melted over its harsh planes and angles, etching its alien virility in ruthless lines. He was a stranger, yet so hauntingly familiar she couldn't stop her hand from lifting, her fingertips from brushing the stubborn jut of his jaw. His eyes were guarded, like the forest at dusk.

"Hello, brat," he said.

Then she felt that old, familiar kick in the stomach and knew she was standing face to face in the moonlit tower with Morgan MacDonnell, his boyish promise of masculine beauty come to devastating fruition.

Mortified by her own boldness, she snatched her hand back, remembering another time she had touched him in tenderness and he had rubuked her in anger.

A wry grin touched his lips. "I suppose if you'd have known it was me, you'd have let me bleed to death."

Terrified she was going to revert to a stammering six-year-old, she snapped, "Of course not. You were dripping all over Mama's Flemish rug."

To hide her consternation, she lowered her gaze back to his hand. That was a mistake for she could not help staring, fascinated by the blunt size of his fingers, the warmth of his work-roughened skin, the rhythmic throb of his pulse beneath her thumb. She had the absurd thought that it must take a mighty heart indeed to fuel such a man.

"You've grown," she blurted out accusingly.

"So have you."

His low, amused tone warned her. She looked up to find his gaze taking a leisurely jaunt up her body, finally coming to rest with bold regard on her face. A splinter of anger twisted in her heart. For so long she had yearned for him to look at her with affection. But why now, when she sensed his admiration might be even more lethal to her than enmity?

Hardly aware of her actions, she tore a strip of priceless Chinese silk from her mother's drapes and wrapped it around his palm. "So what were you doing up here? Plotting a massacre? Trying to find a way to lower the harpsichord out the window? Searching for a mouse to put in my bed?"

Lucky mouse, Morgan thought, but he wisely refrained from saying so. "If you must know, lass, I was searchin' for a moment's peace."

"Ha!" She knotted the bandage with a crisp jerk that finally drew a flinch from him. "Peace and the MacDonnells hardly go hand in hand."

"Fine talk from a lass who just burst in here threatenin' to cut off my head."

Sabrina could hardly argue with the truth of that.

He jerked his head toward the door. "Why aren't you down there with the rest of your family, lordin' your noble gestures over the poor peasants?"

Morgan's size might have changed, but not the rest of him. Resenting his uncanny knack of making her feel ashamed of who she was, she gave a dainty snort. "Peasants, indeed. Barefoot savages, the lot of them. Mama would have been better off serving them at a trough instead of a table."

His voice was quiet, its very lack of emotion a rebuke of its own. "If their table manners aren't to your likin', it might be because most of them won't see that much food again in their lifetimes. And their feet are bare because they're savin' the rotted soles of their boots for the cold winter months. They don't lose as many toes that way."

Shame buffeted her. Sabrina dropped her gaze, then wished she hadn't as it fell on the stark lines of Morgan's bare legs and feet. Golden hair dusted his muscular calves. His soles must be as tough as leather to bear the stony soil of the mountainside without protection. Her own toes curled sheepishly into the plush cashmere of her stockings.

"I begged Mama to let me join the festivities," she confessed.

"Why didn't you appeal to your dotin' papa? As I recall,

he never could resist a flutter of those pretty little lashes of yours."

Sabrina's gaze shot to his face. Morgan had never given her any indication that he'd noticed her lashes before. "Even Papa was adamant this time." A soft chuckle escaped her. "It seems your reputations preceded you. He was terrified one of you might hit me over the head and drag me off by my hair."

Morgan was silent for so long that she feared she'd offended him again. Then he reached down and lifted a skein of her hair in his uninjured hand, rubbing it between thumb and forefinger. A dreamy languor stole across her features. The cadence of Sabrina's heartbeat shifted in warning.

He let the stolen tendril ripple through his fingers in a cascade of midnight silk before turning the dusky heat of his gaze on her. "I can't say I blame him, lass. If you were mine, I'd probably lock you away, too."

If you were mine . . .

The words hung suspended between them, far more awkward than their silence. In a breath of utter lunacy, Sabrina wondered how it would feel to belong to a man like him, dared to ponder what came after being dragged off by her hair.

Caught in the same spell of moonlight and solitude, Morgan's gaze dropped to her parted lips. His starving senses reeled, intoxicated by the scent of roses that flared his nostrils, the cling of her hair against his callused knuckles. He'd long ago resigned himself to the harsh life of a Highland warrior. But this girl's softness awakened old hungers and weakened his resolve. He hadn't touched a drop of wine, yet he felt drunk, reckless. What harm could one kiss to? Resisting the temptation to plunge his tongue between her unwitting lips, he leaned down and touched his mouth to hers.

At the press of Morgan's lips against her own, Sabrina's eyes fluttered shut. His kiss was brief, dry, almost tentative, yet a melting sweetness unfolded within her. She felt the leashed power in his touch. Such gentleness in a man his size wove a spell all its own. Only in the last brief second of contact did he allow himself the wicked luxury of dragging his lips across hers, molding her beneath him in perfect harmony.

TENDER BETRAYAL
by
ROSANNE BITTNER

Bestselling author of OUTLAW HEARTS
and THUNDER ON THE PLAINS

"Bittner's characters are so finely drawn, their lives so
richly detailed, one cannot help but to care deeply for
each of them." —*Affaire de Coeur*

*When Audra Brennan savored her first, forbidden taste of
desire in the arms of handsome lawyer Lee Jeffreys, his
caresses sparked a flame within that burned away the differences between rebel and Yankee.*

The shelling from the bigger guns seemed to have
stopped. She decided that at least until daylight she had no
choice but to stay here as Lee had directed. She went back
to the cot and lay down, breathing his scent on his pillow
and sheets. How odd that she felt so safe in this bed where
a Yankee soldier slept. She was in the center of the enemy
camp, yet she was not afraid.

She drifted off to sleep, losing all track of time. Finally
someone knocked gently on the rear door. "Audra? It's
me."

Audra rubbed at her eyes, holding the shirt around
herself as she found her way to the door. It was still dark.
"Lee?"

"Let me in. The worst is over."

Audra obeyed, and Lee turned and latched the door
again. Audra looked up at him, seeing blood on his right
arm. "You're hurt!"

"Nothing drastic. I told my commander I'd tend to it

myself. He doesn't know you're in here, and I don't want him to know just yet." He threw a bundle of clothes on the small table on which the lamp was sitting. "I looted those out of a clothing store like a common thief. I don't know your size. I just took a guess. You've got to have something to wear when you leave here."

Lee removed his jacket and boots, then began unbuttoning his shirt. "It's a madhouse out there. Most of the men have chased the rebels back into the countryside, and they're looting through town like crazy men. It's practically impossible to keep any of these men in line. They aren't regular army, just civilian volunteers, for the most part, come here to teach the rebels a lesson. They don't know a damn thing about real military conduct or how to obey orders." He glanced at her. "I still intend to have the bastards who attacked you whipped. How do you feel?"

She sat down on the cot, suddenly self-conscious now that she was more rested. She had removed her shoes and stockings and wore only his shirt and her bloomers. "Just terribly tired and . . . I don't know . . . numb, I guess. It's all so ugly and unreal."

"That's war, Audra, ugly and unreal. You asked me once what it's like. Now you know." He peeled off his bloodstained shirt, and Audra found herself studying his muscular arms and the familiar broad chest, the dark hair that lightly dusted that chest and led downward in a V shape past the belt of his pants. He walked to the stand that still held a bowl of water and he poured some fresh water into it, then wet a rag and held it to the cut on his arm, which was already scabbing over. "Some rebel tried to stab me with his bayonet. Missed what he was aiming for by a long shot, but he didn't miss me all together, obviously."

"Let me help you."

"Don't worry about it. It isn't bleeding anymore." He washed his face and neck, then dried off and picked up a flask of whiskey. He opened it and poured some over the cut, grimacing at the sting of it. Then he swallowed some of the whiskey straight from the flask. "They say whiskey is supposed to help ease pain," he said then. "It does, but only physical pain. It doesn't do a thing for the pain in a man's heart."

She looked away. "Lee, don't—"

"Why not? In a couple of days you'll go back to Brennan Manor, and I'll go on with what I have to do, because I'm bound to do it and it isn't in me to be a deserter, no matter the reason. You have to stay near home because it's the only way you're going to know what happened to Joey, and you'll want to be there when he comes home, God willing. Who knows what will happen when all this is over? In the meantime I've found you again, and I need to tell you I love you, Audra. I never stopped loving you and I probably never will."

Audra held back tears. Why was he saying this now, when it was impossible for them to be together? Everything had changed. They were not the same people as they'd been that summer at Maple Shadows, and besides that, it was wrong to be sitting here half-undressed in front of the man she'd slept with while married to someone else, wasn't it? It was wrong to care this much about a Yankee. *All* of this was wrong, but then, what was right anymore?

He set the flask down on the table. "This might really be it, Audra; the end for you and me. But we have tonight."

"Why is it always that way for us? It was like that at Maple Shadows, and that one night you came to visit. All we ever have is one night, Lee, never knowing what will come tomorrow. I can't do that again. It hurts too much, and it's wrong."

Audra looked away as Lee began to undress. "Please take me somewhere, Lee, anywhere away from here."

He came over to kneel in front of her, grasping her wrists. "There *is* no place to take you, not tonight. And it's *not* wrong, Audra. It was *never* wrong, and you know it. And this time it isn't just tonight. When this is over, I'm coming back, and we're going to be together, do you hear me? I'm not going to live like this the rest of my life. I want you, Audra, and dammit, you want *me*! We've both known it since that first day you came here to see me, widow or not! Maybe this *is* the last chance we'll have to be together, but as God is my witness, if I don't get killed or so badly wounded that I can't come to you, I'll be back to find you, and we're going to put this war behind us!"

She looked at him pleadingly. "That's impossible now," she said in a near whisper.

"That isn't true. You just don't want to *believe* that it's possible, because it makes you feel like a traitor." He leaned closer. "Well, then, *I'm* a traitor, too! Because while my men are out there chasing and killing rebels, I'll be in here making *love* to one!"

Why couldn't she object, argue, remember why she should say no? Why was she never able to resist this man she should have hated?

"I never said anything about making love," she whispered.

He searched her green eyes, eyes that had told him all along how much she wanted him again. "You didn't have to," he answered.

THE PAINTED LADY
by
LUCIA GRAHAME

This is a stunningly sensual first novel about sexual awakening set in nineteenth-century France and England. Romantic Times *called it "a unique and rare reading experience."*

This wonderfully entertaining novel showcases the superb writing talents of Lucia Grahame. With lyric simplicity and beauty THE PAINTED LADY will entrance you from first page to last. Read on to discover an exquisite story about a proud, dark-haired woman and her hidden desire that is finally freed.

"If I stay longer with you tonight," Anthony said, his words seeming to reach me through a thick mist, "it will be on one condition. You will not balk at *anything* I ask of you. I leave it to you. I will go now and count tonight to your account, since, although you were occasionally dilatory, you acquitted yourself well enough, for the most part. Or I will stay, on *my* conditions—but at *your* wish. It rests with you. Do I stay or go?"

"Stay," I whispered.

I swayed and jingled as he led me back to the hearthside and laid me down upon the pillows.

"Undress me," he commanded when we were stretched out before the fire. "Slowly. As slowly as you can."

I moved closer to him and began to unfasten the buttons of his waistcoat.

He sighed.

"Don't rush," he whispered. "I can feel how eager you are, but try to control yourself. Take your time."

It was maddening to force myself to that unhurried

pace, but in the end it only sharpened my hunger. As I contemplated the climactic pleasures in store—who could have said how long it would take to achieve them?—I could not help savoring the small but no less sweet ones immediately at hand. The slight drag against my skin of the fine wool that clothed him, more teasing even than I had imagined it; the almost imperceptible fragrance of lavender that wafted from his shirt, the hands which lay so lightly upon my waist as I absorbed the knowledge that the task he had set for me was not an obstacle to fulfillment but a means of enhancing it.

Yet I had unbuttoned only his waistcoat and his shirt when he told me to stop. He drew back from me a little. The very aura of controlled desire he radiated made me long to submerge myself in the impersonal heat and forgetfulness that his still presence next to me both promised and withheld.

I moved perhaps a centimeter closer to him.

"No," he said.

He began, in his calm, unhasty way, to remove his remaining clothing himself. I steadied my breath a little and watched the firelight move like a sculptor's fingers over his cool, hard body.

At last he leaned over me, but without touching me.

"You're so compliant tonight," he said almost tenderly. "You must be very hungry for your freedom, *mon fleur du miel*."

I felt a twist of sadness. For an instant, I thought he had used Frederick's nickname for me. But he had called me something quite different—a flower, not of evil, but of sweetness . . . honey.

He brought his hand to my cheek and stroked it softly. I closed my eyes. Only the sudden sharp intake of my breath could have told him of the effect of that light touch.

He bent his head. I caught the scents of mint and smoke and my own secrets as his mouth moved close to mine.

I tipped my head back and opened my lips.

How long I had resisted those kisses! Now I craved his mouth, wanting to savor and prolong every sensation that could melt away my frozen, imprisoning armor of misery and isolation.

He barely grazed my lips with his.

Then he pulled himself to his knees and gently coaxed me into the same position, facing him.

Keeping his lips lightly on mine, he reached out and took my shoulders gently to bring me closer. My breasts brushed his chest with every long, shivering breath I took.

"You are free now," whispered my husband at last, releasing me, "to do as you like. . . . How will you use your liberty?"

For an answer, I put my arms around his neck, sank back upon the pillows, pulling him down to me, and brought my wild mouth to his. . . .

OREGON BROWN
by
SARA ORWIG

Bestselling author of TIDES OF PASSION
and NEW ORLEANS

"The multi-faceted talent of Sara Orwig gleams as
bright as gold." —*Rave Reviews*

*With more than five million copies of her books in print,
Sara Orwig is without a doubt one of romance's top authors.
Her previous novels have been showered with praise and
awards, including five* Romantic Times *awards and nu-
merous* Affaire de Coeur *awards.*

*Now Bantam Books is proud to present a new edition of one
of her most passionate novels—the story of a woman forced to
choose between fantasy and reality. . . .*

Charity Webster left the city for small-town Oklahoma
to assume the reins of the family company she had
inherited. With nothing behind her but a failed business and a shattered romance, and no one in her new
life except an aging aunt, Charity gives her nights to a
velvet-voiced late-night deejay . . . and to a fantasy
about the man behind the sexy, sultry voice.

But daylight brings her into head-on conflict with
another man, the wealthy O. O. Brown, who is maneu-
vering to acquire the family firm. Arrogant and all too
aware of his own charm, he still touches off a sensuous
spark in Charity that she can't deny . . . and she finds
herself torn between two men—one a mystery, the
other the keeper of her deepest secrets.

And don't miss these heart-stopping
romances from Bantam Books,
on sale in October:

OUTLAW by Susan Johnson

MOONLIGHT, MADNESS,
AND MAGIC
by Suzanne Forster,
Charlotte Hughes,
and Olivia Rupprecht

SATIN AND STEELE
by Fayrene Preston

And in hardcover from Doubleday:

SOMETHING BORROWED,
SOMETHING BLUE
by Gillian Karr

OFFICIAL RULES

To enter the sweepstakes below carefully follow all instructions found elsewhere in this offer.

The **Winners Classic** will award prizes with the following approximate maximum values: 1 Grand Prize: $26,500 (or $25,000 cash alternate); 1 First Prize: $3,000; 5 Second Prizes: $400 each; 35 Third Prizes: $100 each; 1,000 Fourth Prizes: $7.50 each. Total maximum retail value of Winners Classic Sweepstakes is $42,500. Some presentations of this sweepstakes may contain individual entry numbers corresponding to one or more of the aforementioned prize levels. To determine the Winners, individual entry numbers will first be compared with the winning numbers preselected by computer. For winning numbers not returned, prizes will be awarded in random drawings from among all eligible entries received. Prize choices may be offered at various levels. If a winner chooses an automobile prize, all license and registration fees, taxes, destination charges and, other expenses not offered herein are the responsibility of the winner. If a winner chooses a trip, travel must be complete within one year from the time the prize is awarded. Minors must be accompanied by an adult. Travel companion(s) must also sign release of liability. Trips are subject to space and departure availability. Certain black-out dates may apply.

The following applies to the sweepstakes named above:

No purchase necessary. You can also enter the sweepstakes by sending your name and address to: P.O. Box 508, Gibbstown, N.J. 08027. Mail each entry separately. Sweepstakes begins 6/1/93. Entries must be received by 12/30/94. Not responsible for lost, late, damaged, misdirected, illegible or postage due mail. Mechanically reproduced entries are not eligible. All entries become property of the sponsor and will not be returned.

Prize Selection/Validations: Selection of winners will be conducted no later than 5:00 PM on January 28, 1995, by an independent judging organization whose decisions are final. Random drawings will be held at 1211 Avenue of the Americas, New York, N.Y. 10036. Entrants need not be present to win. Odds of winning are determined by total number of entries received. Circulation of this sweepstakes is estimated not to exceed 200 million. All prizes are guaranteed to be awarded and delivered to winners. Winners will be notified by mail and may be required to complete an affidavit of eligibility and release of liability which must be returned within 14 days of date on notification or alternate winners will be selected in a random drawing. Any prize notification letter or any prize returned to a participating sponsor, Bantam Doubleday Dell Publishing Group, Inc., its participating divisions or subsidiaries, or the independent judging organization as undeliverable will be awarded to an alternate winner. Prizes are not transferable. No substitution for prizes except as offered or as may be necessary due to unavailability, in which case a prize of equal or greater value will be awarded. Prizes will be awarded approximately 90 days after the drawing. All taxes are the sole responsibility of the winners. Entry constitutes permission (except where prohibited by law) to use winners' names, hometowns, and likenesses for publicity purposes without further or other compensation. Prizes won by minors will be awarded in the name of parent or legal guardian.

Participation: Sweepstakes open to residents of the United States and Canada, except for the province of Quebec. Sweepstakes sponsored by Bantam Doubleday Dell Publishing Group, Inc., (BDD), 1540 Broadway, New York, NY 10036. Versions of this sweepstakes with different graphics and prize choices will be offered in conjunction with various solicitations or promotions by different subsidiaries and divisions of BDD. Where applicable, winners will have their choice of any prize offered at level won. Employees of BDD, its divisions, subsidiaries, advertising agencies, independent judging organization, and their immediate family members are not eligible.

Canadian residents, in order to win, must first correctly answer a time limited arithmetical skill testing question. Void in Puerto Rico, Quebec and wherever prohibited or restricted by law. Subject to all federal, state, local and provincial laws and regulations. For a list of major prize winners (available after 1/29/95) send a self-addressed, stamped envelope entirely separate from your entry to: Sweepstakes Winners, P.O. Box 517, Gibbstown, NJ 08027. Requests must be received by 12/30/94. DO NOT SEND ANY OTHER CORRESPONDENCE TO THIS P.O. BOX.